BANK JOB

BANK JOB

JAMES HENEGHAN   NORMA CHARLES

ORCA BOOK PUBLISHERS

Library and Archives Canada Cataloguing in Publication

Heneghan, James
Bank job / written by James Heneghan and Norma Charles.

ISBN 978-1-55143-855-9

I. Charles, Norma M. II. Title.

PS8565.E581B35 2009   jC813'.54   C2008-907414-9

First published in the United States, 2009
Library of Congress Control Number: 2008941144

Summary: Thirteen-year-old Nell and her friends are robbing banks to raise
money for renovations in their foster home.

Orca Book Publishers gratefully acknowledges the support for its publishing
programs provided by the following agencies: the Government of Canada through
the Book Publishing Industry Development Program and the Canada Council for the
Arts, and the Province of British Columbia through the BC Arts Council
and the Book Publishing Tax Credit.

Design by Teresa Bubela
Typesetting by Christine Toller
Cover photographs by Getty Images & Veer
Norma Charles photo by Brian Wood

ORCA BOOK PUBLISHERS   ORCA BOOK PUBLISHERS
PO Box 5626, STN. B   PO Box 468
VICTORIA, BC CANADA   CUSTER, WA USA
V8R 6S4   98240-0468

www.orcabook.com
Printed and bound in Canada.
Printed on 100% PCW recycled paper.
12 11 10 09 • 4 3 2 1

To our favorite traveling companions,
Brian and Lucy.

ONE

A wet Tuesday afternoon is as good a time as any for a bank robbery.

Or so I tried to convince myself as I watched through the slanting rain as my friend got ready to rob a Vancouver branch of the Bank of Montreal.

I had a front-row seat.

Down the street in the doorway of Cameron's Shoes, Tom Okada was probably cracking his knuckles while he waited.

Rush hour in Vancouver rushes for twelve hours, from six to six. The traffic on Kingsway was loud and heavy. I checked my watch. It was 2:50 PM. My hands were trembling. I stepped back into the shelter of the doorway as I waited for Billy Galloway to give the signal.

Billy's big, with wide shoulders. He was wearing a blue ballcap, black-rimmed glasses, black mustache and a rain jacket. He tugged at his ballcap, pulling it down firmly on his head. This was the signal. It was time. Billy was going in. It was my turn to move.

My stomach lurched with dread. I felt like throwing up. I couldn't believe I was doing this. Crazy.

Chest thumping, I hurried into the bank and stood at an ATM in the bank vestibule. There was no lineup inside the bank. I counted two customers and two women tellers.

Billy headed toward the younger of the two tellers, the one closest to me. His rain jacket was zipped up over his chin.

He passed a note across the counter:

THIS IS A BANK ROBBERY. YOU WON'T GET HURT IF YOU DO AS YOU'RE TOLD.

I knew what the note said because I had written it.

The teller reading the note wore glasses and looked like she was in her early twenties. Her face paled under her makeup and her hands shook as she reached into her cash drawer and handed over a fistful of bills.

I slipped out of the bank and waited in the rain, my shopping bag ready and my heart racing.

Billy came hurtling out of the bank and crammed his ballcap, glasses, fake mustache and the money into my shopping bag. Then he cut away sharply and disappeared around the corner onto Tyne Street.

I walked quickly in the opposite direction, forcing myself to be calm. Tom Okada, still waiting in the doorway of the shoe shop, grabbed my bag without a word, stuffed it into his backpack and took off in the direction of the SkyTrain station.

I stood in the doorway of the empty shoe shop, knees trembling so much my legs could hardly support me.

The scream of a police siren pushed my panic up a notch. I abandoned the doorway and tried to walk calmly along Kingsway toward the SkyTrain station. The police car swished past me, splashing through puddles, siren wailing.

I stopped, took a few deep breaths and checked my watch: 3:05 PM. No need to hurry, I told myself. I didn't have anything on me that connected me to the robbery. I was perfectly safe. I forced myself to walk calmly and not attract attention. Heart still thumping, I hardly noticed the rain.

There weren't many people on the street because of the rain, but the SkyTrain station was busy. Loosely furled umbrellas dripped onto the platform in widening puddles.

I stepped onto the train, and with a huge sigh of relief, collapsed onto the closest seat.

It had worked! Amazing! I was stunned. We'd really pulled it off.

Eleven minutes later, at 3:16 PM, knees still watery, I got off at Patterson Station.

By 3:32 PM I was hanging my black rain jacket in the hallway at home. There were already two similar jackets there, one gray, the other green.

"Home" was Janice and Joseph Hardy's ancient two-story house on Oliver Avenue, in Burnaby's Patterson Hill area. It had green shingles, white trim and an old-fashioned porch. It was a foster home. Four kids lived at the Hardys'. First there was me, Nell Ford, thirteen. Most people called me Nails. Then there was Billy Galloway, the one who did the actual robbing of the bank. Billy was fourteen. Tom Okada was thirteen, same as me. The fourth kid, Lisa Connors, had been at school during the robbery. She was nine.

Patterson Hill was a good neighborhood, close to schools, close to Patterson Hill Park and close to Metrotown Mall. The neighbors were friendly. They knew that the two-story, green and white house on Oliver Avenue was a foster home.

The Hardys were not home from work yet. Janice worked part-time as a Special Education aide at Chaffey Burke Elementary, from noon to three.

She brought Lisa home with her. Joseph got home from his job in the lost property office at the Public Safety Building at six.

I pulled off my wet shoes and climbed the stairs. Billy and Tom had taken earlier trains and were waiting for me in their room. I sashayed in like a movie star about to take a bow before an adoring audience. They grinned at me, eyes wobbling with excitement.

I felt fine now. My heart was still speeding a bit but the trembling had stopped.

No one said anything until I'd closed the door.

"We did it!" My grin was huge.

"We did it!" yelled Billy, hooting as he bashed Tom with a pillow.

Tom jumped wildly on his bed, doing an excited chimpanzee routine, half crouching, fists dangling at the knees, gibbering and whooping. He grabbed a pillow and walloped Billy over the head. "We friggin' did it!" he cried.

I watched them proudly.

When the boys were tired of the pillow fight, we all huddled together, arms around one another's shoulders, and did a wild victory dance between the two beds. There wasn't much room.

We were the Three Musketeers.

"All for one and one for all," we sang. "All for one and one for all…"

We collapsed onto Billy's bed in hysterics, hooting and laughing.

"Show me the money," Billy said at last, sitting up.

I grabbed the shopping bag from the foot of the bed and emptied it. We knelt on the floor and counted the money on Billy's bed, separating the bills into tens, twenties, fifties and hundreds.

The total came to $1,450.

An astounding success!

Tom cracked his knuckles.

Billy shoved Tom playfully with his shoulder. Tom shoved him back.

We were totally stoked.

The front door slammed. The sound of Janice's voice came up the stairs. "Nell? Boys? Are you up there? I need help bringing the groceries in from the car."

The stolen bills were on Billy's bed. We had to get rid of them fast.

"Be right down," Tom yelled back.

Billy scooped up the money and stuffed it into the shopping bag. "We gotta hide this."

I grabbed the bag. "I've got a place."

"Where?" Tom cracked his knuckles anxiously.

"It's a good safe place. Don't worry."

"You should tell us in case something happens to you," Tom said. "We should know."

I sighed. "Nothing's going to happen to me. Or to the money. We're all in this together. All for one and one for all. Ashes to ashes, dust to dust." I gave them a two-handed closed-fist salute. Then I carried the shopping bag to the room I shared with Lisa. I turned on the light. The Chinese paper lampshade swayed in the draft from the window. Rain peppered the glass.

I shut the bedroom door.

It was easy to tell which side of the room was mine and which was Lisa's. Lisa was a neat freak, and she was cat-crazy. The design on her duvet cover was cats of all colors playing with balls of wool. Her pillow was a white kitten. A cat-shaped lamp sat on her night table. Also on the table was *The Encyclopedia of Cats*. Lisa studied it almost every night like it was the Bible.

My side of the room might have been a bit on the messy side. But it was a comfy mess. I hardly ever made my bed, although Janice kept bugging me about it. Janice had even tried to bribe me by buying me black sheets and pillows and a black-and-white-striped duvet cover. The bribe didn't work though. I didn't see the point of making a bed every day when it just got all rumpled and messed up every night anyway.

One thing Lisa and I had in common was books. I had my battered copy of *Anne of Green Gables* that had been with me since I-don't-remember-when and one or two others, but Lisa had a lot. Her shelves were tidy, her books lined up like soldiers. Even though I didn't own many books, I loved to read. I borrowed some from the library at least once a week.

I had recently read *Pride and Prejudice*. I loved all the old-fashioned language. The girl in the book, Elizabeth Bennet, always said things like, "I am pleased to make your acquaintance," or "I have not had the pleasure of his acquaintance." And if a friend asks her what she thinks of someone she likes, she usually answers, "He is most amiable." Amiable! It just breaks me up. Or she will say an acquaintance is "agreeable," meaning he or she is okay but not quite as good as "amiable." Amiable seems to be top-of-the-line. Third in line is "tolerable." Of course there's always at least one character—the villain—who is "despicable." After taking *P&P* back to the library, I started reading *Northanger Abbey*. Jane Austen rules.

On my night table I had a card that read, *Neatness is the first sign of insanity*. I got the idea when I saw the card on Tom's night table. His card read, *I used to be indecisive. Now I'm not so sure*. The cards summed up our characters pretty well, I thought.

I liked my roommate a lot in spite of her tidiness. I would say Lisa is most amiable. Besides, she's the closest thing to a sister I will ever have.

I opened the closet. Lisa's side was pastel pants and shirts, tidy on their hangers. My side was a jumble of dark sweats, hoodies and jeans from my favorite fashion shop, Value Village.

I knelt on the wooden floor and rummaged under the mound of clothes—mine, of course, thrown out of sight until laundry time—for the shoe box I'd been saving. You never knew when a shoe box would come in handy. Now I had the perfect use for it.

"Nell!" Lisa burst into the room. "Guess what I've got!"

I jumped. I hadn't had time to hide the money. I shoved the bag under the mound of clothing.

Lisa was holding a tiny orange kitten.

Her dark eyes sparkled behind her thick glasses. "His name's Pumpkin. Isn't he the most beautiful? Just feel how soft he is."

I stroked the kitten's tiny head with a finger. It shut its eyes and purred. "Where did you get him?"

"Janice got him from someone at school. You can hold him if you like."

"Hey, you guys," Janice yelled from below. "I said I need help down here. These groceries won't walk in from the car all by themselves you know."

"Okay, we're coming," I yelled back. "Look, Lisa, how about you go and show Pumpkin to Billy and Tom? And tell those guys to go help Janice."

Lisa left. I pulled the bag from under the mound of clothes and transferred the loot from the holdup into the shoe box. Then I grabbed a pen from my desk and wrote the day's score on the lid: $1,450.

I burrowed under the mound of clothes again, feeling for the loose board. I pried it up and dropped the box into my secret hiding place.

There. It was safe.

I heaved a sigh of relief and threw myself onto my bed, trying to relax the tension in my muscles. Let Billy and Tom go downstairs and help Janice bring in the groceries. Janice didn't need all three of us. I was exhausted. The emotional strain of the last few hours had taken a lot out of me.

I sighed. What had I done? I was a bank robber. A real bank robber! There was no way to avoid that fact. I was a criminal.

So much had changed in only one month.

TWO

The social worker's name was Rhoda Mills. She was a cheerful woman who seemed to love her work. She visited us a couple of times a year, always remembering our names. She was in her thirties maybe, with brown hair and glasses that kept sliding down her nose. She kept pushing them back up with one finger.

It was just after four o'clock. Joseph had taken time off work. It was an important meeting. We all had to be there.

Rhoda bustled in and shook hands with Joseph and hugged Janice. Then Janice led Rhoda upstairs and let her take a look at our bedrooms, especially neat and tidy for her visit. We stayed out of the way downstairs. A few minutes later, I heard them talking in the bathroom, also tidied up for the visit.

Inspection over, Rhoda quickly made herself at home. She fetched her bulging briefcase from the hallway and dropped it on the floor beside her chair as she sat at the kitchen table. Soon her papers were strewn all over the table, competing for space with Janice's tea and cookies.

"How are things with you kids?" Rhoda asked, looking mainly at me. "Nell?"

"Things are good," I said.

"How's your mother?" asked Rhoda. "You still see her regularly?"

"Of course," I said. "Weekends, whenever I can. She's fine."

"Billy? Tom? Lisa? Anything new? You kids okay?"

Billy grinned. Tom nodded. "We're great," said Billy. "Right, Tom?"

"Right," said Tom. "We're great."

"Great," Lisa echoed, her face serious.

"Help yourself to more tea, Rhoda," said Janice, nudging the pot toward her.

"Thanks, Janice."

After a minute or two of general chatter, Rhoda looked at me. "Feel free to go, kids. Unless there's anything you want to talk about. Nell?" She raised her eyebrows at us and gave her glasses a push.

"No. Everything's good," I said. We got up from the table.

"That's fine," said Rhoda. "I need to talk with Janice and Joseph for a minute."

$ $ $

"It's so weird hearing someone other than Janice or Joseph call you Nell," Tom said as we headed upstairs.

Janice always called me by my proper name. "Nell is a lovely name," she told me the first day I met her. "And that is what Joseph and I will call you."

"How did you get the nickname Nails anyways?" Tom asked.

"How? You really want to know? You want to hear the story of my life?"

"Not really," said Tom. "Just the Nails part."

"Well…" I took a deep breath. "If you really want to know…I've lived in fosters all my life…"

"All your life? You've got to be kidding."

"It's true. Ever since I was a baby. Most were okay, but the one before I came to the Hardys' was gruesome…"

"Gruesome?"

"Gruesome. Are you gonna keep repeating everything I say?"

"Sorry."

Lisa went to our room to read while the boys and I headed into their room. I settled into the beanbag chair, and Tom and Billy lounged on their beds.

"It was run by an old cow named Mrs. Osberg—the kids called her Iceberg—who beat us with a cane—"

"She beat you with—"

"With a cane, yes. If you interrupt me one more—"

"Sorry. I'll shut up. Promise."

"She beat us if we did anything she didn't like. She was new at fostering. It was obvious she wouldn't last long. Once the social worker found out what was going on, that would be the end for her. I was always in trouble with the old bag and got most of the canings. On the backs of my legs usually."

Tom nodded. "So it wouldn't show."

"Huh? Right. Anyway, I refused to do Iceberg's laundry one day. 'Do your own filthy laundry!' I told her. She got mad, grabbed me by the arm and beat me with her cane. I didn't cry. 'You little trollop!' she yelled at me. 'You're hard as bloody nails.'"

"She sounds like a monster," said Tom.

"She was. After that, the other kids started calling me Nails. Then everyone was calling me Nails. I kinda liked the name."

"Suits you."

I smiled. "Thanks."

Tom nodded again. "Nails are hard, but they're sharp and they're tough, and no matter how much they get battered they always keep their heads. That's you all right—Nails. Hard as."

Except for the interruptions, Tom was a good listener. I liked the way he analyzed stuff, especially the bit about keeping my head. Billy didn't say anything, but I could tell he was listening. He was pretending to read a comic book, but he didn't turn the page once.

"After another beating one day," I continued, "I decided to live up to my new name. I kicked Iceberg twice—bam-bam—both shins."

"Sounds like the old cow deserved it."

"That's what I thought. She collapsed shrieking on the floor. I was scared, but in a way I was glad. I had proved I could be hard as nails if I wanted. No more quiet Nell Ford who took what the bullies handed out. I was Nails. I was tough. I would never let anyone boss me around, ever again. Just let them try. Iceberg was shrieking and writhing on the floor like a rubber monkey, and I ran away, slamming the door behind me. The police found me in a bus shelter late that night. Social Services closed old Iceberg down and sent me here, and I've been here ever since."

Tom said, "Wow!"

I grinned. "So that's the story."

"That was amazing. Remind me never to tangle with you, Nails, okay?"

$ $ $

Janice called us downstairs for a family meeting when Rhoda had gone. She and Joseph were sitting together at the kitchen table looking totally grim.

"Kids," Janice said, "we've got some bad news."

"What's up?" said Tom.

I said, "Is there a problem?"

I remembered that there was a small problem way back when I first came to the Hardys', when the ministry ordered Joseph to get the old-fashioned wooden bedroom windows fixed. "Children need fresh air," the social worker had said—this was the one we had before Rhoda. I don't remember her name. The problem was that the old wooden windows wouldn't open because they had a million coats of paint on them. So Joseph spent a whole weekend fixing them and then sent a form to the ministry showing that the work had been done.

We sat. Joseph opened a bottle of beer. I watched how the muscles in his forearm moved. Joseph wasn't a big man. Billy was a few inches taller, but Joseph looked solid and strong. What I liked most about him was that he didn't preach. He never got up on a soapbox to lecture us. Janice, sitting beside him, was a calm motherly woman with strands of gray showing in her dark hair. She was smart too. She didn't lecture us either—well, not very often. They loved each other. Anyone could see that. "We married when we were in our teens and still wet behind the ears," Janice always said, laughing. They wanted kids, but it never happened.

We were their kids, their family.

Joseph sighed as he looked at us. "There's new ministry regulations since the last time Rhoda was here."

Billy groaned.

Lisa, following Billy's lead, groaned also.

Joseph said, "One of the new regulations has to do with hygiene…"

"Bathrooms," said Janice.

"We don't have enough," Joseph said. "With six people in the house, we need…"

"…two full bathrooms minimum," Janice finished.

"Preferably two point five," said Joseph.

I looked at Billy. Billy looked at me. I knew what he was thinking: The ministry was right. We really didn't have enough bathrooms. There was a full bathroom upstairs—tub, shower, sink, toilet—but only a toilet and sink in a small powder room downstairs. The house was built a zillion years ago.

But so what? I thought.

"We manage okay," I said. "Usually anyway."

"Not good enough," said Joseph. "This has come up before. We were warned last year that there were going to be new regulations. So we checked with the…"

"…Foster Parents Association," said Janice.

"And there was nothing they could do to help," said Joseph. "The new rules are…"

"…here to stay," said Janice. "We're not the only ones. We've been given six months to comply."

"What's comply?" asked Lisa.

Janice said, "Right now, darling, it means we need an extra bathroom."

I said, "What happens if we don't get it?"

Janice looked at Joseph.

Joseph shrugged. "The ministry will reduce the number of kids allowed here…"

"…to one or two," Janice finished for him.

"What!" said Tom. "You mean at least two of us would have to friggin' leave?"

"Break up the family!" I cried.

"I'm afraid so, Nell," Janice said.

We all groaned, Billy, Tom, Lisa and me.

Not another foster, I thought. Not another move. Not when it was so perfect here. Not when I'd finally found a family where I belonged.

I was shattered.

"Friggin' ministry!" said Tom.

"No good blaming the ministry," said Janice. "They only want what's best for kids."

Joseph said, "Janice and I already looked—a few months ago—into the possibility of having…"

"…the downstairs toilet remodeled," said Janice.

We brightened up.

"That's it," said Tom. "Remodel the downstairs bathroom. No problem." He looked at Billy eagerly. "Right, Billy?" Then he looked at me. "Nails?"

Joseph said, "We'd need to make room for a tub and shower."

"How could you do that?" I asked.

"We figured to knock out the wall of the hall closet and put up a new wall where the closet doors are," said Joseph. "Only problem is the expense—building materials, plumbing supplies and so on. Brent Murphy is a local contractor. He came and took a look. He reckoned it would cost us about…"

"…ten thousand dollars," said Janice, "including the new tub and shower and all the fittings."

Tom said, "Ten friggin'…You're kidding!"

Joseph shook his head.

Janice said, "It's ten thousand dollars that we don't have right now."

"So what you're saying," said Tom, "is that at least two of us will have to leave and get sent somewhere else, and we'll be split up for sure."

Silence.

I looked at Billy and he looked at me. Tom was busy cracking his knuckles, and Lisa was about to cry—I could tell from the way she was wrinkling her nose. I squeezed her arm, and she leaned into my shoulder.

Janice said, "We've got six months to come up with a solution." She shrugged.

We stared at each other.

Leave Janice and Joseph?

Deadly.

I knew how I felt, and I knew how the others felt. Our whole world was about to fall down around us.

No one wanted to leave the Hardys'.

No way.

I would do just about anything to stay.

Anything.

Janice looked at all of us. I could tell she was crushed. "Now kids," she said, "I don't want you to worry too much. Joseph and I—"

"We're going to do everything we can," said Joseph.

"We didn't tell you to make you worry," said Janice. "We just don't…"

"…want any secrets in this family," said Joseph.

$ $ $

That night, Janice came upstairs to tuck Lisa into bed as she usually does. She looked tired. There were wrinkles between her eyes that I hadn't noticed before.

She sat on the edge of Lisa's bed, smiling at both of us. "I don't want you two to worry," she said. "I'm sure everything will work out."

"But what if it doesn't work out?" Lisa asked, sniffing, trying not to cry.

"Let's worry about that if it comes. We've got six months to think of something."

"I don't want to leave here," said Lisa. "Not ever. I don't want to leave you and Joseph, or Nails and the boys. You're my family." Her face crumpled and tears glistened in her dark eyes.

"I know, Sweetie Pie," said Janice, rubbing her back. "And we don't want to lose you either. You talk to her, Nell," she said as she was leaving. "Try to make her see that things will work out—one way or the other."

Lisa cried.

I felt like crying too. Our family was about to be annihilated.

There had to be something we could do. There just had to be.

We had to stay together.

THREE

I got the idea for the Musketeers the next night while we were watching an old movie from Joseph's video collection. It was our usual Friday family night, with chips, popcorn and root beer—the works. The Three Musketeers, loyal seventeenth century swordsmen, fought for the king of France. I remembered reading the book and loving it. The movie wasn't as good as the book, but it was good—especially all those hot guys in capes swishing their swords around. It was a change from our favorite gangster stories, old black-and-white films starring Humphrey Bogart and James Cagney.

Billy and Tom liked the *Musketeers* movie too. We even watched all the extras. I loved their slogan, *All for one and one for all.* Loyalty and friendship.

Cool! If only we—Billy and Tom and I—could be like the Musketeers and fight for Janice and Joseph and Lisa. And for ourselves, of course—we didn't want to break up the family. Nobody wanted to be carted away to some foster horror home.

That was when the idea hit me. Why couldn't we try to raise the ten grand for the extra bathroom? The three of us. The Three Musketeers.

Why not?

$ $ $

The next morning I was still thinking about the Three Musketeers and at least two of us having to leave the Hardys'.

Everyone was up early. Tom helped Janice make waffles while Lisa and I did our usual Saturday chores, stripping the sheets and pillowcases off our beds and getting the wash started. Billy helped Joseph with outdoor chores, fixing the back fence and sweeping leaves off the front walk. Janice called us all when breakfast was ready.

Janice and Joseph were quiet, not their usual cheerful selves. We were pretty quiet too. All except Billy. His face was flushed and his appetite was as good as ever. He even drained the dregs from the bowl of sliced fruit Janice served with the waffles.

After breakfast Janice took Lisa out for a haircut. She wanted me to come with them, but I had decided to grow my hair out.

Billy said to me and Tom, "Wanna take a walk up to the park?"

I could tell he had a plan and I wanted to find out what it was, because I had a plan too.

There was no rain, but there was a damp chill in the air. We grabbed our rain jackets. Janice, on one of her shopping sprees—she called them shopping seizures—found them at The Bay's winter sale for less than half price. Mine was black, Tom's was green, Billy's was gray, and Lisa's was red. Except for the colors and the sizes, they were identical.

Patterson Hill Park was at the end of the block, a short walk from the house.

We settled around a picnic table.

Billy sat on the table, feet on the seat. He obviously had something on his mind. He would have something damp on his behind if he sat there for too long. I did a few leg stretches, leaning against the table.

The park at that hour on a Saturday morning was busy with walkers and joggers. Tom bounced his basketball impatiently, frowning at Billy. He should have known better than to try to rush him. Billy always took as much time as he needed.

Finally Billy said, "So what do you guys think we should do about this extra bathroom business?"

"Huh? There's nothing we can do," said Tom. "Not so far as I can see anyway." He tossed his ball from one hand to another. "I agree with the regulations. One bathroom for six people is ridiculously unsanitary. I used to have my own bathroom. All to myself. With a shower and a whirlpool tub. Four bathrooms we had altogether, three of them en-suite, for three people, can you believe it? That was before my mom and dad…" He stopped.

Silence.

Billy looked at Tom. "So you don't mind leaving the Hardys'?"

Tom said nothing. I couldn't see his face because he'd turned away from us.

I said, "I bet there's something we can do. We could be like the guys in that movie last night, the Three Musketeers, working together, all for one and one for all. We could go out and get what we need. I bet we could raise the ten thousand."

Tom turned to me, annoyed. "Ten thousand bucks! It might as well be a million! We're just kids. How can we raise that kind of money? Sell raffle tickets, maybe? Pet and babysitting? Dog walking? Yeah, right. Sometimes, Nails, I think you're friggin' brain-damaged or something."

Brain-damaged. I felt my insides shrink. A giant hand squeezed my heart.

Billy looked at me and nodded slowly. "Nails is right. There is something we can do."

I smiled up at him. At least Billy didn't think I was brain-damaged.

"Oh yeah?" said Tom.

"I've got a plan," said Billy.

"What kind of plan?" said Tom.

Billy said, "The way I see it, the only way we're ever gonna get the kind of money we need is…" He paused, looking at me, then at Tom.

"Is?" Tom said, kicking the picnic table impatiently. "Is what?"

"Steal it," said Billy.

"What?" Tom's dark eyebrows disappeared under his spiky black hair.

"Funny," I said, but I didn't laugh. "Tell us another one, Billy."

"I'm serious," said Billy. "I've thought it all out. We need to be like the Three Musketeers. Nails is dead right. We need to go out and take what we need."

"What?" Tom stared at Billy. "No way. I hate the friggin' idea. You won't catch me stealing. Besides, the Three Musketeers never actually stole anything, did they?"

"Yes, they did," said Billy. "They stole from the bad guys and gave to the good guys."

"No, they didn't," said Tom. "You're getting them mixed up with Robin Hood."

"No, I'm not."

"Yes, you are."

"The Musketeers gave to the good guys."

Tom said, "Didn't you watch that video last night? Were you awake? They weren't stealing money. They were protecting the king. Tell him, Nails."

"We'd be protecting the family," Billy said before I could open my mouth. "Same thing."

"You're so full of crap," Tom said. "Stealing is for losers. Everyone knows that."

"Just who were you thinking of stealing from?" I asked.

"The bank," said Billy, casually checking out his fingernails.

Tom's jaw dropped. For once he was speechless.

Billy smiled his slow smile.

"The bank?" I said. "You're kidding, right?"

"No, I'm not kidding. The bank is the obvious choice. It's the place with all the money."

Nobody said anything. Billy stomped his long legs on the picnic table's seat, grinning at us like a happy Buddha.

Then he said, "Think of Joseph's old gangster movies. Think how easy it is. You walk into a bank, you tell them it's a holdup, and you walk out with their money. Remember Edward G. Robinson in—I forget the title—and Steve McQueen in that St. Louis movie? And Gene Hackman in *Heist*?"

"But they had guns and knives. Or something serious and scary," I said. "And besides, they're only movies, not real life."

"Sometimes bank robbers have a note. Just a note. No weapons." Billy made his voice deep and scary. "A note and a scary voice."

"You'd never get away with it," Tom said. "You're a total lunatic."

"But we would. My plan is foolproof. The reason bank robbers get caught is because…gather round while I give you a lesson in advanced physics."

Tom stared.

"Bank robbers get caught," said Billy, his voice lowered, "because they don't work together like pickpockets."

"Pickpockets?" I said. "What do pickpockets got to do with it?"

"And what's advanced physics got to do with it?" asked Tom.

Tom was a straight-A science student.

Billy answered Tom. "Advanced physics is the universal movement of bodies and particles. Matter and energy."

"So?"

"For us, money is the matter and we're the energy." He turned to me. "A pickpocket is smart. As soon as he steals a wallet, he hands it off to a partner faster than the speed of light. His partner then disappears. That way, if the mark feels his wallet being lifted and he grabs the pickpocket, or if the police catch him, the pickpocket looks innocent because he hasn't got the wallet. Get it?"

Tom said, "I get it all right. It's not advanced physics, it's advanced garbage. Your mind has snapped, Billy. Totally snapped."

"There'd be nothing to it. We could raise the ten grand in no time flat. Don't you see?"

"No way." Tom shook his head. "I don't want to hear any more."

With that, he stomped away like he wanted to crush every worm and bug in the rain-soaked turf.

Billy called, "No point going off mad, Tom. Come back and talk. Be reasonable."

Tom hesitated. I could see he was trying to decide what to do. Finally he shook his head and came back. He stood, hands on hips, unconvinced, waiting to hear what other craziness Billy had to deal out.

But I spoke first. "Tom's right, Billy. It's nice of you to try figure out a way we can all stay together with the Hardys, but kids robbing banks makes no sense, no sense at all."

Billy shrugged at me and smiled.

When Billy smiled at me like that, I'd do anything for him. A spurt of happiness gushed through me. My heart skipped and my face flushed. As Jane A. would say, Billy was an exceedingly amiable young man.

Then he smiled at Tom as well.

Tom shrugged and looked down at his shoes. "Sometimes, Billy," he said quietly, "I think you ought to be in a lunatic asylum, not in a nice sane place like the Hardys."

Billy laughed and looped an arm round Tom's shoulders, and we all walked back to the house together.

FOUR

MARCH 11

A whole week had gone by, and we hadn't come up with any other ideas for raising the money. Tom had spent some time on the phone, but judging from his tight lips, I didn't think he'd managed to scare up the necessary funds.

Billy tried talking us into his crazy bank-robbing scheme again, but we told him to shut it. His smiles and persuasive manner weren't working.

Ten grand was on my mind. I had an idea Mom might be able to help out.

My mom is Carolina Ford. She lived less than an hour away in a co-op apartment on False Creek in Vancouver.

I set off to visit her. The SkyTrain was crowded, and I had to sit beside an old geezer who was reading *The Province* newspaper.

I don't like old geezers. I was in a foster once that had an old geezer in it. That one, I don't ever want to think about. I tried to think about something else.

Money. I thought about money. Lots of money. Billy wanted us to rob banks. Tom hated the idea. It was risky and dangerous. If my idea worked out we wouldn't need to steal.

I watched the Burnaby landscape flash by. A seat on the other side of the train became vacant so I moved. The old geezer stared at me over the top of his paper. Tiny pig eyes.

Like Elizabeth Bennet, I definitely wouldn't wish to make his acquaintance. He was not an amiable person at all—probably a despicable one.

I ignored him. I could see the distant towers of Vancouver.

I got off at Granville Station and took a bus to False Creek. My mom's co-op apartment is on Commodore Road, close to the seawall and a short walk from Granville Market.

I walked up the sidewalk edged with bright green ferns and colorful spring flowers—even if it wasn't quite spring yet—and I let myself in with my own key. Mom was watching TV in her bathrobe, as usual, with a can of Coke in her hand, also as usual.

Zero activity and sugary drinks were making her plump.

"Hi, Mom. How are things? Did you remember to eat breakfast?" A quick glance around the messy apartment told me all I needed to know.

Maybe Mom and I were alike in lots of ways.

My mother is mentally handicapped.

I have trouble convincing myself sometimes that I'm not mentally handicapped too. Take school. Except for English, I'm pretty hopeless. I hardly ever get things right, especially in math. Most of my grades are awful. I'll be glad when I don't have to go to school anymore.

Mom's got the mind of a child, even though she's an adult. She is able to take care of herself only with the help of social service agencies. But she's sweet and always cheerful.

I sat beside her on the sofa and gave her a big hug. She hugged me back.

I got up. "I'll scramble some eggs. Your favorite. Would you like that? Scrambled eggs? And toast, if there's any bread. Just relax. Breakfast will be up before you can say 'as the stomach turns.'"

Mom watched soaps most of the day, from *The Young and the Restless* in the morning through to *Guiding Light* in the late afternoon. I've watched them with her ever since I was a little kid, with the social worker supervising until I was twelve.

So far, Mom had said nothing. She just watched me with her happy baby smile. But now she said,

"Don't trouble yourself about breakfast, Sweetie. I'm not so hungry."

"It's no trouble. You don't feel hungry because of all that sugar water you're swilling. After you've had breakfast, I'll do your hair. Would you like that? Would you like me to do your hair?"

Mom's hands flew to her dark hair, thick and tangled. "Oh, would you, Nell? I'd like that an awful lot. I love you doing my hair."

Mom was almost forty. When she was twenty-four, she married John Ford, also mentally handicapped. Then they had me, their first and only child. My father worked at the corner gas station at the time.

I was taken away from them after only a month, because the government said they were incompetent parents. Social service agencies tried to help them care for me, but it was no use. When it came to babies, Carolina and John didn't know what was the top and what was the bottom. They went to the Dairy Queen or the movies and left me alone. I was left unwashed and unfed for hours while my mother watched TV. She didn't understand. She thought babies cried to exercise their lungs or something.

The neighbors blew the whistle on them.

How do I know all of this? Because I read the newspaper story years later.

There was a court hearing.

The paper said the new baby (me) was in danger and should be removed to a place of safety. That's how they put it: "removed to a place of safety."

The experts described the baby (me) as "a normal little girl with normal potential." I never believed that. I mean, how can two mentally handicapped people have a normal baby?

Anyway, the judge decided baby Nell (me) could not stay with her parents. The danger to her health and happiness was too great, he said.

My mother cried all through the hearing. All she knew was that they were taking her baby away from her.

I kept a copy of the article as a memento of sorts. It was on the front page of the *Weekend Sun* under the headline:

TRAGEDY WITHOUT EVIL—RETARDED PAIR
FORFEITS BABY

Retarded pair.

No one says *retarded* now. Things have changed in thirteen years. Now they say "intellectually challenged" (yech!) or "mentally handicapped," which I like better.

I've read the newspaper story over and over. I know it by heart, every word. It was a long time before I could look at it without crying.

$ $ $

Mom was talking to me, something about her hair.

"Sorry, Mom. Was I pulling? I swear it's grown two inches since the last time I cut it."

Mom giggled. "Has it really, Nell? Has it really?"

I was pretty good at doing her hair. I was taking off about half an inch using the kitchen scissors.

"So dark and thick," I said. "It's easy to see where I get mine."

Mom's head swiveled around. "And your lovely green eyes, Nell. You got your eyes from me too, don't forget. Don't forget your lovely green eyes."

"Keep your head still, Mom. You wouldn't want me to cut off your lovely pink ear now, would you?"

Mom tensed, frightened.

"Kidding, Mom, only kidding."

She relaxed and I massaged her head and brushed her hair.

"Mom, could I ask you about your pearl necklace?"

Mom thought for a few seconds. "The beautiful pearl necklace my mother left me?"

"Yes. Will it be mine some day?"

"Yours? Of course it will be yours, Sweetie. After I'm gone, everything will be yours. My music box with the little dancer. And my book of stickers from

Expo 86. And my picture of your daddy on duty at the gas station in his smart uniform with the stripes. It was taken just a month before he died, you know. I remember I was out at the park that day." She smiled her child smile at me. "Everything will be yours."

"Could I see it, the necklace?"

Mom looked confused as she tried to remember where she kept it. "See it now, you mean?"

"Yes, Mom. See it now."

"Is my hair finished?"

"Come and see in the mirror. It looks great."

$ $ $

On the SkyTrain home, I hooked Mom's necklace out of my jeans pocket and let the beautiful pearls run through my fingers.

She wouldn't miss it. I hadn't taken the box.

Even if Mom opened the box and saw it empty, she wouldn't remember anything. She would start looking for the necklace under the furniture. Thing was, it was really mine, in a way. I mean, she planned to give it to me.

I got off at Metrotown Station.

Ten minutes later I was in the mall, leaning over the counter of Pearson's Jewelers as a bald geezer took the necklace from me.

"How much is it worth?"

He reached for his eyeglass but stopped and smiled without even using it. "It's costume jewelry."

"What do you mean?"

"They're not real pearls."

I didn't say anything.

He examined the necklace. Then he took the eyeglass out again. "I'm sorry," he said, "but this is worth very little." He shrugged apologetically. "Thirty dollars maybe. Certainly no more than fifty."

Fifty dollars! I slid the pearls back into my pocket.

"Thanks very much," I said, and took off fast, expecting to hear the old geezer laughing at me, the mentally retarded kid.

FIVE

The next day, a windy afternoon in Patterson Hill Park, the three of us gathered around our usual picnic table. Beds of bright daffodils shook their yellow heads madly in—what—sprightly dance? Is that what the poet said? Except the daffs weren't dancing, they were shaking their heads at us as fast as they could go. "No. No. No." That should have told me something.

"You have to do it, Billy," I said. "You have to go in and hand the bank teller the note. You're the biggest. You could pass for eighteen, maybe nineteen."

"That's what I figured." He grinned.

Billy had convinced me that the only way we'd ever get our hands on such a huge amount of cash was to go along with his robbery scheme.

I said, "You could get the money, then get out of the bank real fast, and Tom could be waiting—"

"Not me," Tom shook his head. "No friggin' way. Forget it. Look, I've been thinking."

"You got a better idea?" asked Billy.

"You could say that," said Tom. "At least it won't land us in jail for the rest of our lives."

I said, "What's your plan, Tom?"

"There's a trust fund set up for me. I'm not allowed to touch it for…well anyway, I could try and get…"

I felt like hugging him. "Oh, Tom, that'd be so wonderful." I turned to Billy. "Wouldn't it, Billy?"

Billy looked disappointed. "Yeah. Sure it would."

$ $ $

Billy waited a few days before asking Tom about the money. We were on our way home from school.

"Well? Did you get it?"

Tom looked at the cars speeding by in the street. He said nothing for a while. Then without looking at us, he said, "Couldn't get it. There's money for university but nothing else. Not till I'm twenty-one."

I could tell Billy was trying his best not to look pleased.

$ $ $

The next Saturday, we spent an hour shooting hoops at Patterson Hill Park. It was windy and cold. We took a break and sat at the picnic table.

"So what's it to be, Tom?" asked Billy.

Tom stretched himself out on one of the wooden seats. "If you're talking about what I think you're talking about, the answer's still no."

Billy turned to me, sitting on the other seat. "Looks like it's just you and me then, Nails."

I shrugged.

Billy came over and sat beside me, with his back to Tom.

"So it's back to my plan. I pull the holdup, okay?"

"Okay," I said, "then I'll take the handoff. You think it will work, Billy? You really think we can get away with it?"

Billy smiled. "Trust me. I don't see how it can fail."

Billy filled me with hope. I trusted him. He made anything seem possible. If he said we were going to jump over the moon, I'd believe him. We would get the money for the extra bathroom. None of us would have to leave the Hardy home after all.

I appealed to Tom. "We need you as part of the team, Tom. If there's three of us, we'll be like the Three Musketeers. All for one and one for all."

Tom sat up and shook his head. "Friggin' brain-less, I call it."

Brainless. There it was again.

I turned to Billy. "Okay, Billy. It's just you and me. So I'm standing there with the bag of money. Now what do I do?"

But Billy wasn't giving up on Tom. He walked over to the other side of the table and laid a hand on Tom's shoulder. "I'm thinking it would be safer to have a second handoff, Tom. We really need you, bud."

Tom stood, shaking his head. I could see he didn't like saying no to Billy. He looked up at him. It was hurting Tom to refuse.

Silence.

"So I'm standing there with the bag of money. Now what do I do?" I asked Billy again.

Billy's usually sleepy face was flushed with excite-ment. He turned away from Tom and said to me, "You walk down the street, all calm like, to where Tom is waiting."

I said, "But Tom…"

"Don't worry. Tom will change his mind. He won't let us down. As I was saying, you slip Tom the bag. We all head for the SkyTrain separately, taking our time and being sure to take different SkyTrains. We don't want anyone catching us together. It'll work. It's got to."

Billy's a pirate at heart, I'm sure of it. He's a buccaneer. No one but us, his best friends, would ever guess from his sleepy appearance that deep inside he longed so much for adventure, excitement and danger.

I swallowed. "If it means keeping all four of us together," I said, "I'm game." We knocked fists.

"I knew I could count on you, Nails." Billy smiled his gleaming smile, and my stomach did a flip.

Amiable just doesn't cut it. Billy's perfect, pure and simple.

We headed back to the house. Tom was quiet. Billy is big, at least six feet tall with broad shoulders. He sort of rolled as he walked. Way cool.

"You know what?" I told him. "From the back you even look like a bank robber. You're like the bank robber in that old black-and-white western we saw, I forget his name…"

He turned around and grinned. "Billy the Kid."

"That's the one."

Billy Galloway was a kid on life's skateboard, having himself a good time.

"Were you thinking of some kind of disguise?" I asked. His face with its freckled nose and ruddy cheeks looked too young for a bank robber. It wasn't just the freckles and cheeks, it was something else. Maybe the long curly hair that hardly ever saw a comb, or maybe the happy twinkle in his blue eyes.

Billy said, "Disguise? Fake mustache maybe?"

"What about some glasses with black frames? I got a pair from Value Village. I thought they'd make me look older, but they're too big for me."

Billy nodded. "Fake mustache, glasses, maybe a cap to hide my hair. That should do it."

Tom didn't say anything. Like the daffodils at the park the week before, he shook his head in worried disbelief.

SIX

We spent the rest of the weekend trying to persuade Tom to join the team. The thing was, except for us—me, Billy and Lisa, and the Hardys, of course—Tom was totally alone. Both his parents were dead; he had no other relatives. We were his only family, his only friends.

Tom came to the Hardy house last September, a year or so after Billy and me. It was his first foster. He's the same age as me but wasn't in any of my classes at Moscrop Secondary. He was in the gifted program and I wasn't. You had to look for me in the Learning Center getting help with math.

On Sunday night Lisa was in bed with a sore throat, so I hung out in the boys' room. Billy and Tom were finishing their homework. I didn't do homework. I was relaxing in their window seat, enjoying the romantic problems of Catherine Morland in *Northanger Abbey*.

Billy put down his book and stretched. "So I've got our first bank all picked out."

"I friggin' told you," said Tom, "I'm not robbing any bank."

"You'd rather leave it to chance that you'll be shipped off to some insane foster?" I asked. "You don't know what they're like, Tom. Some of them are really gruesome."

"Yeah," said Billy, "it's crazy the kind of places they think it's okay to send you."

"What do you know about crazy?" Tom asked.

"More than you, I bet," said Billy.

"I friggin' doubt that," said Tom. "I know all about crazy."

Tom rarely talked about his life before the Hardys. Janice told us Tom's parents were dead, but that's about it. We knew his mom had died of cancer, and for the longest time all he would say about his dad was that he went funny. Billy and I didn't bug him for details. Lots of kids don't like talking about the reason they're in a foster home.

"I lived with crazy for a year," said Tom.

"Your dad?" I asked.

"Yeah," said Tom. "His doctor said it might be the beginning of Alzheimer's. That's the disease where your brain starts to get holes in it like Swiss cheese, you know?"

I nodded.

"But I looked it up on the Internet. Dr. Anderson was wrong. My dad didn't have Alzheimer's. Alzheimer people forget every friggin' thing. They forget where they live, forget what year it is, forget their names, everything. Dad didn't forget important stuff.

"I think he just missed Mom so friggin' much. He stopped going to the office and worked in his garden instead. He was building a shrine to Mom. You should've seen it—azaleas, maples, bonsai trees, a pond with koi and a waterfall, lanterns hanging outside a miniature ceremonial teahouse. An authentic Japanese garden."

"Sounds nice." I loved the words Tom used. No wonder he was in the gifted program.

"I liked being in there and thinking about my mom. It felt like she was close by, you know?"

I nodded.

"But then my dad stole a garden gnome from the neighbors. He put it in the center of the garden, next to the waterfall. Now, have you ever seen a Japanese garden with a gnome in it? Have you?"

I could tell I was supposed to be horrified. "You've got to be kidding!" I said.

"Right! It's like dropping a greasy hot dog into the center of a perfect platter of sashimi. I asked him why he was doing it. Now get this: He said, 'Beauty is in the eye of the beholder, my son. I have created a harmonious marriage between North American popular culture and ancient Japanese art.' It made no sense.

"But that wasn't the end. My dad brought home more garden gnomes and even pink flamingoes and a jockey. Then he brought home all kinds of gardening tools—shovels and forks, electric hedge clippers, hoses, an electric lawn mower and a full set of patio furniture until the backyard could hold no more. The beautiful Japanese garden disappeared under all the junk. Then the house began to fill up with odd things like realty and election signs, garbage cans, doormats, lawn chairs, children's bicycles, wagons, go-carts— on and on.

"Eventually, someone in the neighborhood called the police. They came and looked at everything, and they scratched their heads. They didn't know what to do. The neighbors said they didn't care about their stuff. The poor man had just lost his wife. He was sick and didn't know what he was doing."

"You had nice neighbors," I said.

"So the police contacted Social Services. A mental health guy started visiting once a week. You want to hear the supreme irony?"

I wasn't sure what irony was, supreme or otherwise, but I said, "Sure."

"During one of the talks with the health worker, my dad had a heart attack and died."

Okay, I got irony—the opposite happened to what was supposed to happen. A health worker is supposed to make you healthy. But you die. Funny. I thought Tom was trying to make it funny to cover how upset he was. You laugh to keep yourself from crying.

I said, "Sounds to me like your dad just wanted to be with your mom. He must've really loved her a lot."

"Yeah."

Billy said, "I'm sorry you had to deal with that, bud. It is pretty crazy. Nobody should have to deal with that."

Tom gave Billy a sideways smile of thanks.

"That's why we have to stick together," I said. "So we don't have to deal with the crazies anymore."

"True enough" said Billy. "That's why we need to get cracking."

"I just don't think it will work," Tom said. "You'll be arrested for sure. Or even killed. Whoever heard of kids trying to rob a friggin' bank?"

"Just because we're kids doesn't mean we can't do it," Billy argued. "I keep telling you, we've got this foolproof plan. We get the money, do a couple of handoffs, and we hop on the SkyTrain. What could be simpler? Worst case scenario, we're caught. What can they do to us? We're kids. We're too young to be thrown in the slammer. They don't send kids to jail. Slap on the wrist is all we'd get."

Tom said, "Slap on the wrist? What do you mean?"

Billy grinned. "When you're kids, they go easy on you. Pick up the garbage for a week, something simple. Or maybe a few days in juvie."

"What's juvie?"

"Juvenile detention center, of course. Don't you know anything?"

Tom still wasn't buying. His voice climbed. "Look, Billy. I like it here. But I don't plan to spend the rest of my teens in a friggin' detention home!"

"Thing is, if we don't raise the ten grand, and soon," said Billy, "living here with Janice and Joseph won't be an option."

"You don't want to even think of what's out there passing for fosters," I told Tom, shuddering. "And out there is where we'll end up. Don't you see?" I stared at him hard and said slowly, "We just don't have any other options."

Tom was quiet for a long time, doing homework, but I could tell his mind wasn't on it.

After a while he threw down his pen and turned to Billy. "You sure I wouldn't have to go inside the bank?"

"I'm sure," said Billy. He flashed his most charming smile. "You just grab the bag from Nails, then stroll to the SkyTrain station. No need to run. Everything's cool. Simple? Yeah! The Three Musketeers! All for one and one for all." He held up his fists. "Are you in?"

Billy knew how to generate excitement all right.

Tom looked at me. Then he looked at Billy. Then he nodded. "Okay, I'm in."

Billy flashed him another of his sweet smiles. "That's my buddy!"

Tom was in. Yes!

"But we can't tell anyone," I said.

"Right," Billy said. "No one. Not even Lisa. It's top secret."

"Let's swear an oath of secrecy," I said. "Say 'Ashes to ashes. Dust to dust. We're the ones that you can trust.'"

Billy said the oath loud and clear, and Tom mumbled along.

"Now say after me," I ordered. "All for one and one for all."

We knocked our fists together and then held them up, chanting, "All for one and one for all. All for one and one for all."

That was how it all started.

It was history.

SEVEN

APRIL 4

So there we were after our first perfect bank robbery. Billy and Tom were sitting at the kitchen table after lugging grocery bags from Janice's car.

"Hey, Janice, you sure snapped up a lot of stuff," said Billy, peeking into one of the bags.

Janice rolled her eyes. "I had a shopping seizure. There were so many specials my brain had a burnout." She started packing food into the cupboards.

It was my turn to help. I loaded milk and yogurt into the fridge. "Lisa's kitten is cute," I said.

"Luckily, they had a special on kitty litter, so I got three bags." Janice turned. "Tom, Billy, the kitty litter is still on the backseat, and there's a pack of toilet paper as well."

Tom and Billy got up and slouched back out to the car.

I frowned. "Is a kitten a good idea for Lisa? What if we have to move?"

Janice sighed. "That's a bridge we'll cross when we come to it."

She looked so sad at the thought of losing her family that I felt like telling her right then and there to stop worrying. That Billy and Tom and me, we were taking care of it. But I remembered our oath to secrecy: *Ashes to ashes. Dust to dust.* So I kept my mouth shut.

Tom staggered in with a huge bag of kitty litter, Billy close behind him with another, carrying it easily on his shoulder. They added the bags to the pile on the floor beside the counter. Then Tom reached up and punched Billy on the shoulder.

Billy punched back. Soon the two of them were wrestling and giggling around the kitchen table. A chair toppled over. Billy pounded Tom in the stomach. Tom squirmed and pounded him back, and they chased each other, a small and panting David and a big giggling Goliath, around the kitchen.

"Knock it off, you two! Look out for the groceries!" Janice yelled. "Someone could get hurt. Bring in the rest of the stuff from the car. Nell, you and Lisa can set the table for supper." She looked out the window at

Billy and Tom. "I don't know what's got into those two boys lately, especially Billy."

"What do you mean? What's wrong with Billy?"

"Oh, I don't know. He's different lately—hyper. Like somebody left him a million bucks or something." Janice stopped packing and looked at me. "He's not doing anything he shouldn't, is he?"

My heart rode a plunging elevator down to my ankles. "Like what?"

"That's it. I don't know. He seems to be on a high. He hasn't met a girl, has he? Anything like that?"

I laughed and threw my arms around Janice in a hug. "Billy's fine. Don't worry about him. I would know if there was anything wrong, and there isn't, okay?"

"Well, Nell, if you say so." She pecked me on the cheek and went back to storing groceries. "You probably know him as well as anyone."

$ $ $

It was Joseph's turn to say grace, which he did with bowed head. "Thanks, Lord, for the family and the food. Amen."

"Amen," I said with the others.

"Okay, let's eat." Joseph started passing the food along the table.

I liked the way Joseph always said grace before meals. He was sincere. Not like some of the geezers and old ladies in my other fosters who prayed a lot and talked about God and hellfire and then turned around and…

The thing about Joseph and Janice was that they were completely upfront. They said what they meant and meant what they said. The Hardy home was the first place where I truly felt part of a real family. They didn't have a whole lot of money, but they never stinted when it came to taking care of us. They would give us the shirts off their backs, as the saying goes. We all ate the same food, no favorites. But most of all they were affectionate, a new experience for me, and they treated us like we were special and important in their lives.

It was a squeeze with the six of us around the kitchen table. Janice's smile went around like a lighthouse beam. "Eat up, everyone," she said. "Enjoy!"

I slurped up some noodles. Tomato sauce dripped down my chin and onto my T-shirt. Messy me. Good thing the T-shirt was black. I mopped it up with my napkin.

"Nails," Tom said, "the proper way to eat spaghetti is to twirl it around your fork like this." He gave a demo.

"You can use your spoon to help if you want," he said with one of his superior smiles.

Everyone, even Billy, stopped eating and watched Tom's demonstration. Then they all stared at me. I felt my face turning red. I hate it when people stare at me. I felt like a freak in a circus sideshow.

Sometimes Tom was so prissy, he made me want to puke.

Seriously.

I pulled a face at him.

Janice came to my rescue. "Nell is hungry, that's all." She smiled at me. "Eat up, kiddo," she said.

Somehow, I wasn't hungry anymore. My appetite had been squelched.

I was practically a failure at school, and now I couldn't even eat spaghetti properly, according to Mr. Pain-in-the-butt-perfect Tom Okada. I glared at him and picked at a meatball.

He pissed me off sometimes. He's so smart, straight-A student, math guru, physics genius. I'd heard him at school debating with his nerdy friends about something called string theory, not to mention particle theory, black hole theory, and quacks and quinks theory. Pain-in-the-butt theory is what he's best at if you ask me.

When supper was over there was nothing left of the spaghetti and meatballs. As I cleared the table, I covered my plate with the salad bowl so Janice wouldn't notice I'd eaten practically nothing.

$ $ $

Lisa took Pumpkin into bed with her.

I told her, "Pumpkin sleeps in his box on the floor."

"But why can't he sleep with me? He's so tiny. What if he gets cold during the night?"

"There's a warm blanket in his box, remember? He'll be fine."

"But what if he's lonely all by himself?"

"He won't be lonely. We're right here if he needs us."

"But…"

"Sweetie, a kitten needs to be trained. Janice says the way you start him off in life is important."

"Is it okay if I just hold him while you read to me? I'm sure he'll like the story of the Golden Fleece."

"Yes, but when we're finished he goes right back into his own bed, okay?"

I often read to Lisa at bedtime. We were working our way through a book of ancient gods and heroes. She liked reading on her own, but she liked it more if I read to her.

She was slated for an operation in a month or so. She'd had a lot of really bad sore throats all winter, so the doctor said her tonsils should come out.

She was worried. It was the idea of going to hospital. She had never stayed in a hospital before.

I didn't blame her for being worried. Hospitals can be scary.

She had been with the Hardys the longest of all of us, at least three years. After her parents died in a boating accident when she was four, she was sent to live with a foster family who made her sleep in a dark scary basement all by herself. That was probably why she hated sleeping alone. Also they had an older daughter who was mean to her. After a couple of years, the mother in the family got sick, so Lisa ended up at the Hardys'.

Janice told me that Lisa's mom and dad had come from El Salvador as refugees. Lisa probably inherited her beautiful, black, curly hair from her mom. Janice said that Lisa's grandfather in El Salvador was really old and there was no one else to look after Lisa, so she became a foster kid.

"Do you remember your mom and dad at all?" I asked her.

"Not much." She started to shake her head but stopped and held her head really still like she didn't want to disturb a memory. "Sometimes in the night, I wake up and I can remember a nice warm feeling, like I'm sitting in my mom's lap. It's so warm and soft and she's hugging and kissing me and I'm snuggling right in. Sometimes when I smell a certain kind of flower, I get that cozy warm feeling too.

Maybe that's how she smelled. Real sweet, like that flower maybe?"

"What about your dad? What do you remember about him?"

"He used to give me rides on his shoulders, and it felt so safe up there with him holding my legs tight. I could see everything, like I was the boss of the world, or the queen of England, or something..." Her voice trailed off and she buried her face in the kitten's fur.

She looked so sad. I wanted to cheer her up.

"Let's see if Jason will ever find that golden fleece," I said, opening the thick book and patting a spot on the bed next to me.

Lisa cuddled close to me as I started reading.

"I don't ever want any of us to move from here," she whispered to me after I finished the story. She tucked the sleeping kitten into his bed, and then she tunneled under her quilt.

"Don't worry, Sweetie," I told her as I went to turn off the lights. "None of us will ever have to move. Not if I can help it."

EIGHT

The next day, we were still riding high on the roller coaster of success after our first robbery. We were ready for our next triumph. But first we had a meeting in the boys' room.

"Everything worked perfectly," said Billy. "And we took almost fifteen hundred big ones."

He was on his bed, leaning against the headboard, hands behind his head.

Tom was sitting on the floor near the window working on a Sudoku puzzle. "Hey!" he said. "Fifteen hundred bucks means we'll need to do seven robberies to meet our goal."

"No problem," said Billy, with a shrug.

I stared at him. "It's an awful lot of robberies, Billy.

I don't know if I can keep it up. I thought my heart… Weren't you scared?"

He laughed. "Not a bit. I knew I had you two backing me up. What could go wrong? There was no danger to me. No security guard, nothing. It was a piece of cake. A yummy slice of mocha chocolate layer. I enjoyed it."

"Enjoyed it? You're crazy!" I didn't believe him.

Billy laughed again.

I couldn't decide how much of his enjoyment was real and how much was put on for our benefit.

"What about you, Tom?" I asked. "Weren't you scared?"

Tom's initial delight had disappeared. "Not really. By the time I got the bag the thing was just about over and done. But I still don't like the idea of going to jail."

Billy looked at him. "Look, the banks we pick are going to be small ones, right? No big banks with crowds of people. And it's not like we're breaking into the vault to steal a million bucks. We take small bites only. We're minnows, not sharks. They don't know there's been a robbery until it's over. You won't be seeing the inside of a jail, trust me. It's perfectly safe. Two handoffs. Two different bags. Everyone on the move. Foolproof. Look, you did a great job, Tom. Be proud of yourself."

Billy turned to me, sprawled on an orange beanbag near the door. "You too, Nails. You did a fantastic job."

I blushed with pleasure.

$ $ $

I fought that night with Tom—tangled with Tom.

He'd said he didn't want to tangle with me ever, but it seemed to me he needed a reminder.

It wasn't the boys' turn to use the bathroom first; it was mine and Lisa's. But Tom pretended to forget. He did that sometimes. Once he was in there with the door locked, there was nothing Lisa and I could do but wait. And wait.

His excuse was that he didn't like going in after me because I left a mess, hairs and toothpaste and a wet floor. So he said. But he exaggerated. I wasn't any worse than anyone else.

The house's one-and-a-half bathrooms for six people often led to temper tantrums—shouting and yelling, thumping, door-slamming.

Joseph and Janice had rules. Rule number one: maximum time in bathroom at bedtime—ten minutes. There was a digital clock beside the mirror. Rule number two: everyone left the room tidy for the next person. Rule number three: we took turns for who went in first. Girls' night, boys' night.

But tell Mr. Tom Okada that.

When Tom came out and saw me glaring at him, he went all innocent. "Wasn't it our turn? I could've sworn you guys were first last night."

We yelled at each other for a while. We tangled.

I was the first to quit.

What was the use? Tom would never change.

He wasn't courteous, like me. Or amiable. Sometimes he was quite despicable.

NINE

APRIL 6

Holdup number two was the Toronto Dominion Bank. There were only a few people in the bank—three customers and maybe four bank staff.

It was raining. I was standing outside the bank entrance, heart hammering same as last time. I had my foot in the door as Billy slouched up to the counter in his disguise. I could hear his harsh scary voice but couldn't make out the words.

The teller was young. She freaked out.

"Help!" she screamed. "Help!"

Everyone froze, including Billy.

Then he turned and ran, pushing through the door and dumping his disguise into my shopping bag. It all happened so fast I didn't have time to think.

As Billy disappeared around the corner, my legs went weak and I almost fell to the ground. But I took a deep breath and pulled myself together. Had anyone seen Billy ditch his disguise? Expecting to feel a heavy hand on my shoulder any second, I clutched the shopping bag to my chest and walked casually—though I was shaking like a paint-mixing machine—to the children's toyshop where Tom waited.

Without a word, he grabbed my bag and quickly stuffed it into his backpack. Then he headed toward the SkyTrain station. I looked around. Everything was quiet. People were walking by like normal. No angry mob running out of the bank.

I headed for the train station, too frightened to look over my shoulder.

$$\$\ \$\ \$$$

Half an hour later, we met in Billy's and Tom's room.

Billy grinned. "Was that scary or what?"

I collapsed into the orange beanbag. "That girl screaming scared me half to death. It was a bummer."

"Friggin' bummer!" said Tom, cracking his knuckles. He glared at Billy. "So your plan isn't exactly foolproof, Billy."

Billy shrugged. "I meant foolproof against getting caught. We weren't caught, were we?"

Tom sulked. I said nothing.

Billy said, "There's not much I can do if someone freaks out. She was a cuckoo bird, that teller."

"You looked scary and you sounded scary, Billy," I said. "Maybe that was the problem. It was like a horror movie. What if you just smiled nicely and spoke in a normal voice? The girl wouldn't have been so terrified and she wouldn't have screamed."

Billy laughed. "But I need to scare them a little," he said. "Maybe I should pull a crazy face, go cross-eyed or something."

"It's not funny." Tom slid off his bed and lay on the floor by the window, stretching himself out. "We didn't make a nickel on that robbery, not one cent. In fact, if you factor in the cost of the wear and tear on our shoes, we lost money."

Billy stared at the ceiling and said nothing. He looked relaxed and at peace with the world. Holdup number two had been a failure. But so what? I knew what he was thinking: There was always a next time.

Tom started jerking his arms and legs, as though trying to shake poison from his limbs. Then he sat up and stared out the window at the SkyTrain tracks. "This reminds me of something my dad used to say."

"What's that?" I asked him.

"It's an old Japanese proverb. 'Taste everything, but swallow only what tastes right to you.' And I'm telling you guys, this whole thing tastes downright foul to me." He pounded the windowsill with his fist and then continued staring out the window.

I couldn't look at Tom's slumped sad back another minute. I went to my own room to lie down and close my eyes. I was shivering. I crawled into bed.

And worried.

What were we doing? Where would it end?

I pulled the covers over my head, the girl's terrified scream still echoing in my ears.

TΣN

Tom admired and respected Billy. He always had, right from the beginning.

When Tom first started school, some of the other kids bullied him. Why? Who knows, but Tom had three possible strikes against him: he was small, he was a total nerd and he was Japanese Canadian. There are always racists. You can't get away from them. And there are always bullies. Do I sound like I'm fifty years old? Well that's the way I feel sometimes.

My best friend at school was Liesel Fischer. Liesel noticed Tom being bullied at lunch hour one day. She pointed out Brad Stoker and Frank Drake, well-known tenth-grade morons, at the edge of the field picking on Tom Okada. I told Liesel that Tom was the new kid at my foster, and we ran over to help him.

Tom had been standing, rigid with anger, fists clenched. I yelled at them to pick on someone their own size. All that got me was an earful of insults. It seemed to affect Tom though. He threw himself at Drake, but he didn't get far because Stoker tripped him. Tom fell to his knees.

Liesel and I jumped in. She aimed a blow at Stoker from behind and it connected with the back of his neck. Stoker spun around and punched Liesel's shoulder. She reeled backwards. I tried to kick Drake, but I missed as he stepped away, sneering at my incompetence. Tom tried to stand, but Drake pushed him over with his foot. Tom scrambled to his feet and threw himself once again at Drake, but Drake punched him hard in the stomach. Tom doubled over, gasping.

That was it. They were too big and too strong for us. Their punches and slaps were more than we could handle. I grabbed Tom, and the three of us ran off as Drake and Stoker hollered insults at us.

That night I told Billy what had happened.

He listened. We never saw much of one another at school, me and Billy, because we had our own friends. "Leave it to me," said Billy quietly. "I'll see what I can do."

Tom and I did the dishes after supper the next night. Tom had this thing about scrubbing pans.

He hated it more than anything. I didn't care, so I washed and he dried and put away.

Once the clatter of dishes, pots and pans made it hard for anyone to overhear, Tom said, "Our friend Billy is some piece of work."

"What do you mean?"

"You should've seen the way he scared the crap out of those two guys who picked on me yesterday."

"Drake and Stoker?"

"Who else?"

"What did he say to them?"

Tom grinned. "It was great. They were calling me names again—you know, the usual kind of stuff—when Billy comes over and grabs them by their jacket collars."

"By their…?"

"I was stunned. He had them in a real tight grip, up round their necks, choking them almost, one in each hand. It was like King Kong coming out of the jungle and catching a couple of noisy monkeys. Billy lifts both of them up at the same time. So they're dancing on their toes, and he says real quiet like, 'Don't like to see you messing with my pal, see.'"

"Wow!"

"He lets them go and they—"

"You're slowing down. Keep drying," I said. "Then what happened?"

"They fall to the ground, and then they stagger around trying to suck air into their lungs. When they're finally able to speak, Drake yells, 'You gonna be sorry you did that, mountain man.' Stoker goes, 'I'm telling the vice-principal you almost killed us, fag.' Billy goes, still real quiet and calm, 'Get lost, jerks. You bother my friend one more time and I'll rip your stupid heads off.'"

"That's what he said? He'd rip their stupid…?"

"That's exactly what he said."

"Wow. That Billy! What did they do?" I asked.

"Nothing. They were too scared. You should've seen their faces."

"I bet."

"Then we just walk off and leave them there, spitting and gasping. It was unbelievable. You should've been there, Nails. You would've fractured your ribs from laughing so hard."

As far as I knew, Brad Stoker and Frank Drake left Tom alone after that, which was one of the reasons we loved Billy so much.

And why Tom decided to go along with robbery number three.

ELEVEN

"We haven't hit a Royal yet, have we?" Tom asked Billy nervously. Crack-crack with the knuckles. We were sitting in a half-empty SkyTrain carriage, traveling from Burnaby to New Westminster.

Only a week had gone by since our first holdup, and already this was our third.

Billy had a hit planned on the Royal Bank close to the Columbia Street SkyTrain station.

"I wish you wouldn't do that, Tom," Billy complained mildly.

"Do what?" asked Tom.

"Play with your bones," said Billy. "Every time you crack your knuckles it reminds me of what we've got inside us. Bones. Blood. Guts. Yuck." He shuddered.

"Sorry," said Tom.

Billy answered his question. "No Royal Bank. Not yet. We've hit a Montreal and a Toronto Dominion. This will be our first Royal, right, Nails?"

I nodded. "Right."

"Equal opportunity bank robbers, that's us," said Billy, flashing his buccaneer grin.

Tom cracked a knuckle. Billy groaned.

"Sorry."

$ $ $

We followed our usual plan.

I was worried. What if a teller screamed again, and we had to make a run for it? I didn't think I could take another scare like that.

There was the usual rain.

Tom waited in a doorway about twenty paces from the bank on the same side of the street.

Billy and I headed for the bank. It was a small bank, recently updated to include a vestibule with two ATMs. Billy pulled on the handle of the heavy glass door. An automatic opener took over and the door swung outward.

I followed him inside and we stood at the ATMs like we were about to use them. I took a look around. No security stiffs. But we already knew that from checking out the place a few days ago.

There was only one customer. No lineup. Three tellers, two of them available, a youngish man and a woman. I hoped Billy would choose the woman even if there was a chance she might scream like the last one. Men played violent video games and believed in Superman. Men were aggressive wannabe heroes. Men could be dangerous. The woman had a friendly face.

I hated this part, the seconds before the robbery. My stomach ground like a cement mixer, and I wanted to throw up. Not Billy though. He loved it. Out of the corner of my eye, I saw Billy peel away from my side. He didn't say anything before he left. The rule was silence.

Billy walked up to the young teller with the pleasant face. The sign on her counter said, *Customer Service Representative*. I felt bad that we had to scare her. I had to remind myself that I was Nails. Hard as. Plus, we were doing this for an excellent cause— keeping the family together.

A woman with a baby and a toddler was fussing with the hood of the baby's stroller, preparing to go out in the rain. The toddler looked up at me with enormous brown eyes. I held the door open for them, then left the vestibule and waited outside, shopping bag ready, heart pistons hammering like an engine in a five-ton truck.

Seconds later, the job was done. Billy, relieved of his money and disguise took off toward the SkyTrain station. He was clean. There was nothing to connect him with the robbery.

$ $ $

As I moved away from the bank with my shopping bag, I was guessing that the blood pumping through Billy's pirate veins and arteries was a Niagara of happiness.

I wished I could feel the same.

I made my silent handoff to Tom, cramming my bulging bag into his backpack.

I was clean. I took a deep breath of relief.

Tom headed to the Columbia SkyTrain station, taking his time.

I waited a few minutes, listening for the wail of the police siren, before strolling toward home in the rain.

I had a pounding headache.

$ $ $

When I got home, I flicked off my shoes and coat and headed straight upstairs to the boys' room. It was warm in there and smelled like dirty socks. Billy was sitting cross-legged on his bed. He took a big bite out of an apple.

"Show us the money," he said, grinning and munching his apple at the same time.

Tom pulled the bag out of his backpack and emptied it onto Billy's bed. Flutter of bills.

I counted it.

"How much?" Tom cracked his knuckles.

"Four hundreds, eight fifties, fifteen twenties and two tens."

I tried to do the math in my head.

"The total is eleven hundred and twenty dollars," genius Tom said.

"Not bad," Billy said, eyes gleaming.

"Not bad," I said.

"Friggin' right!" Tom said. Crack-crack.

There was no celebration this time. We'd become seasoned professionals. But we bumped fists. "All for one and one for all!" we chanted.

"Great job, team," said Billy.

I went to my room, lifted the floorboard, dropped the bills into the shoe box, and wrote the amount on the lid.

The Three Musketeers had scored another victory.

So why did I feel so rotten?

TWELVE

The next day after school, Billy, Tom and I were shooting hoops at the park with Larry, a short grade-eight kid from school. It was Tom and me against Billy and Larry, two on two.

The ball was cold and gritty in my hands. I bounced it a few times and aimed for the basket.

Tom had another idea. "Pass it," he yelled at me. "Come on, Nails. Pass it over here."

Larry came at me waving his skinny arms in my face.

I lobbed it over his head in Tom's direction. It went way wide.

Tom missed and frowned. I knew he was swearing at me under his breath.

Billy grabbed the ball and lobbed it toward the basket. It swished right in.

"Ten!" Billy shouted, raising his arms, a grin stretched across his face. He and Larry high-fived and danced around the court.

"If Nails would learn to friggin' pass…," Tom grumbled.

"You think you're so great? You missed more shots than you got in," I yelled back at him.

"Well at least I shoot at the basket sometimes," he yelled at me.

Tangling with Tom yet again.

"What do you think I was trying to do before you started yelling at me?" I said.

"Girls can't jump!"

"And nerdy boys can't either!"

"You know what you can do? You can go and…"

I bounced the ball and ignored him, trying not to hate him. That pain-in-the-butt Tom Okada complained way too much. He was always on my case. According to him, I couldn't do one single thing right—couldn't play basketball. Couldn't even eat spaghetti right. All according to fancy Mister Tom Okada's fancy rules.

Larry said he had to go. "Me too," I said. I grabbed my bag off the bench. "See you guys later."

"Good game," said Larry, smiling as he fell in beside me.

"Yeah," I muttered. "Good game."

I said good-bye to Larry at the park gates and headed for home. White petals from the cherry blossoms whirled around my feet like snowflakes. I kicked them up into a cherry blossom blizzard.

The front door was not locked. I let myself in.

I heard Janice and Joseph talking in the kitchen.

I sat on the bottom step in the front hall and untied my running shoes.

"Look at this, Joe," Janice said. "The Bay is looking for full-time workers. I could apply. I'm sure I'd make more than I do at the school."

"Then you wouldn't be here for the kids. They need you here when they get home," Joseph's voice rumbled. "They've had enough neglect in their lives. Being here for them after school is the least we can do."

I heard the rustle of newspaper. "You're right," Janice said. "Of course, you're right. What about the bank? Have you heard anything on the mortgage?"

"They said no. As we thought they would. We don't qualify for a second mortgage..."

"What about your brother? Ron is rolling in it. I bet if you asked him, he'd help us out."

"I called him last week. He's going through a hard time himself right now. No extra cash. Everything's tied up in some deal. I hated asking him."

"Oh, Joe, what are we going to do?"

"I don't know, Hon. I just don't know."

They both sounded so sad. I wished I could bounce in there and tell them they didn't need to worry. That Billy and Tom and me were getting the money. It wouldn't be long before we would have the whole ten thousand. But I couldn't say a thing.

Lisa's kitten bobbed out of the living room and danced toward me, tiny claws clicking on the hardwood.

"Hey, Pumpkin," I whispered, scooping him up and nuzzling his furry back.

"Is that you, Nell?" Janice came from the kitchen, her usual bright and cheerful self. "You're back."

"Got tired of shooting hoops," I told her. "Going up to my room to read for a while."

I carried the kitten up to my room. It was extra tidy, even my side. Janice had supervised bedroom cleanup that morning. She even made me make my bed. She had become a lot fussier about tidiness since Rhoda's visit. Maybe she thought if everything else was perfect, they'd let her and Joseph keep us all here, in spite of the bathroom problems. Fat chance.

Lisa was at a friend's for the afternoon, so I had our bedroom to myself. I shut the door, dropped Pumpkin onto my bed and patted his head. I went to the closet and dug around for the loose board. I pried it up and reached inside for the shoe box. There were three entries on the lid so far.

Bank 1—$1,450

Bank 2—$0

Bank 3—$1,120

There was a total of $2,570 so far.

We still had a long way to go.

I slowly counted the money, smoothing out the bills, stacking them into a neat pile, hoping the total would be higher. It wasn't. It was too far away from the ten thousand dollars we needed. This robbing banks deal was not working very fast. At the rate we were going it would take a whole year before we had enough.

We didn't have a year. We had only a few months.

THIRTEEN

APRIL 13

Billy chose the small Scotiabank in Surrey Place Mall, only a block from the SkyTrain station.

The mall was busy with shoppers. "Should work in our favor," Billy explained. "It'll be easier to make our getaway in the crowd."

I was standing in the doorway of the Boston Pizza, opposite the bank.

Tom was waiting over at the ice-cream shop further along the mall. I figured he'd probably be cracking his knuckles as usual. He never said much about being anxious or scared, but I knew he was.

Billy headed into the bank, ballcap pulled down low over his forehead as usual. Also as usual were glasses, fake mustache, jeans, gray jacket zipped over his chin.

I moved closer and stood outside the bank. But I couldn't wait. I followed him inside. I knew that wasn't the plan, but I couldn't stand not knowing what was going on. Tom wouldn't be able to see us. His job was to wait.

I got into the bank in time to see Billy pass his note to the teller, an older woman with big hair. I edged closer so I could hear.

"Touch the silent alarm and you're dead meat!" Billy growled at her.

She froze with fright.

"Gimme all your bills and be quick about it!"

When I saw the terrified teller reaching into her drawer, I left quickly and waited outside, holding my bag ready.

Billy came rushing out, dumped everything into my bag and took off.

A man came running out of the bank. He didn't notice me because of all the people walking by.

"Stop thief!" he yelled.

Billy turned sharply right, into Shoppers Drug Mart. The bank man rushed in after him.

Trouble.

I hurried over to the ice-cream shop and made my handoff to Tom. He stuffed my shopping bag into his backpack and then disappeared into the crowd of shoppers, heading for the SkyTrain station.

The whole operation, from bank robbery to final handoff, had taken less than two minutes.

I hurried back to Shoppers Drug Mart. If the man from the bank caught Billy, we could be in real trouble. The bank man was big and athletic. I got there in time to see him leap on Billy and wrestle him to the floor. They upset a display of sunglasses, the bank man on top of Billy, yelling like crazy. I felt helpless. What could I do? I fought the urge to rush over and try to pull the bank man away from Billy.

A counter clerk, just a kid, helped the bank man to his feet. The bank man's eyes were snapping with excitement. "He just…robbed the bank," he panted, pointing down at Billy with a trembling finger. "Call the police."

The store manager pushed through the gathering crowd. "What's going on here?"

"This hoodlum just robbed the bank," said the bank man. "Call the police."

"Call the police," the manager ordered the clerk.

The clerk spun away toward the phone.

Billy climbed to his feet, stunned. "I gotta go," he said.

"You will stay right here until the police arrive," the bank man said angrily, clamping two big hands onto Billy's arm.

The manager, on the other side, gripped Billy's elbow with both hands. Billy struggled, but the two men were too much for him. They led him away to the office at the back of the store. I followed at a distance, lurking by the door, pretending to check out the vitamins.

What could I do to cause a distraction so Billy could get away? Maybe knock down the vitamin display? I tested it. It was bolted to the floor.

"Sit here," the manager said to Billy, pointing to a chair.

Billy sat, looking puzzled as he brushed his hair out of his face.

They waited.

I waited.

My heart was pounding. My mouth was dry.

A police officer finally arrived, an experienced, older man, who began by questioning the bank man. "How do you know this kid robbed your bank? Did you see him?"

"Yes, I did. Gloria—Miss Hampton—sounded the silent alarm after she handed over the cash from her station. I saw him leave the bank. I chased him— didn't take my eyes off him for one minute—into the store here and caught him."

The police officer took the bank man by the arm and whispered loud enough for me to hear, "But this is just a big dopey kid. Are you sure he's the one you saw?"

"Yes, I'm sure. He was wearing a disguise, and I recognize his raincoat."

The police officer ordered Billy to stand up.

Billy stood.

The police officer said, "How old are you, son?"

Mumble-mumble.

"Speak up."

"Fourteen."

The police officer turned to the bank man. "What are they feeding kids these days—dinosaur meat?" He turned back to Billy. "This man said you robbed his bank. Well? Did you rob his bank?"

Billy looked shocked. "No, sir. This man assaulted me. He is making a big mistake. The store clerk over there is a witness. Jumped on me and wrecked my back." Billy twisted and groaned with the pain of it.

"I'm going to search you," said the police officer. "Empty your pockets."

Billy, bent in pain, emptied his pockets.

The police officer searched him. Then he shook his head and looked at the bank man and the store manager. "No cash. No disguise. Did you see the kid with anyone, a partner?"

I held my breath. Had the bank man seen me outside the bank with my shopping bag?

But the bank man looked bewildered. And so did the manager. One shrugged. The other shook his head. The manager said, "Sam might've seen something."

"Get him in here," growled the police officer.

The manager called the clerk in. "Was this kid alone when he came into the store?"

Sam shook his head. "I didn't see him running in. I didn't see nothing. All I seen was this guy"—he pointed at the bank man—"jump this guy." He pointed at Billy. "And knock over the sunglasses display."

"You're my witness," Billy said to Sam. "You saw this man deliberately attack me, right?"

Sam stared up at Billy nervously. "I...I dunno."

The police officer turned to the bank man. "How can you be sure the thief came into the store? How do you know he didn't just keep running and get lost in the crowd?"

The bank man frowned. Before he could answer, the police officer said, "Did you lose sight of the thief at any time? Between the time he left the bank and the time it took you to get out into the mall? Did you have him out of sight, even for one second?"

The bank man said, "No, I told you. I didn't take my eyes off him." But he was beginning to look worried.

"Could you be mistaken? The kid here, well, you can see for yourself. He's got no money, no disguise. Could the real thief have got away?"

The bank man said, "But…"

I had seen and heard enough. Billy would be okay. He didn't need any help from me. I headed for the train station.

$ $ $

"They let me go," Billy explained later to Tom and me in their room. "I gave them a false name and address. Then they let me go."

I asked, "What name and address did you give?"

Billy chuckled. "Thomas Cruise, fourteen-zero-eight Magnolia Street."

"I felt awful watching them question you," I said, "and not able to help. How is your poor back? Are you still in pain?"

"Nothing wrong with my back. I just wanted to freak out the guy from the bank."

"No more holdups," Tom said firmly. "That's it for me. You guys want to rob friggin' banks, well, you go right ahead, but count me out. I quit!" He cracked his knuckles. "Thomas Cruise, Magnolia Street! Was that dumb or what? You were almost caught! And if they get you then they get us too. I don't plan to spend the rest of my life in prison."

Billy shrugged. "I already told you. They don't send kids to prison."

I said, "Stop it, you two. How much did we take this time?" I pulled the shopping bag out of Tom's backpack, emptied it onto his bed and counted the bills. There weren't many. "A hundred and fifty dollars."

"One-fifty," moaned Tom, disgusted. He snatched the bills and threw them to the floor. "All that stress and all we get is hundred and fifty friggin' bucks!"

We always expected thousands, many thousands. In gangster movies, bank robbers were always counting huge stacks of crisp hundred-dollar bills. A hundred and fifty dollars didn't even come close. A hundred and fifty dollars, in the opinion of Tom Okada, was a joke.

I agreed with him, but I didn't say anything.

"I quit!" he said again. "The whole idea is friggin' stupid!"

"It's not stupid!" I said. "We're the Three Musketeers, remember?"

"The Three Musketeers is stupid and you're friggin' stupid too!" Tom left, slamming the door.

$ $ $

Later that night Tom and I were in the kitchen doing the dishes. He said angrily, "Billy talks us into it. We do whatever he says. It's like we're his puppets. He pulls the strings and we jump."

"Not me," I said. "Nobody pulls my strings. I go along with him because he's right. It's the only way we can ever get our hands on that kind of money."

Tom snarled, "You look into his big blue eyes and listen to his voice and you're lost. It's like hypnosis. He's charismatic, that's what he is. Well I can resist him. It's not a problem for me. But you, you're…"

I didn't listen to the rest. I didn't need any more of Tom's criticism. Turning my back on him, I buried my hands in the suds and scrubbed the pots hard. I finished the dishes, and I was out of there.

$ $ $

Billy talked to Tom. Charmed him. We were walking to the bus stop on our way to school.

Billy looped one big arm round Tom's skinny shoulder like Tom was the best pal he ever had. "You know, Tom, a hundred and fifty bucks isn't all that bad. It's more lettuce than I ever saw before we started this caper."

"Billy's right, Tom," I said.

Billy said, "I know it's a small amount compared to the ten thousand we need, but we'll get there eventually. If we keep at it. If we don't give up."

"Sure we will," I said.

"But…," said Tom.

Billy cut in. "It's like playing in the top of the seventh and you're a run down and the other side's got all the bases loaded. What do you do? You don't give up. You get in there and pitch, that's what you do. You get in there and you pitch until you drop. It's never over till it's over."

Tom said, "Yeah?"

"You're a good buddy, Tom. The kind of buddy I'd want on my side if things ever went wrong. You're like a brother. All I want is for us all to stay together at the Hardys', you and Lisa and me and Nails. We're a family, right? The only family any of us has, right?"

Tom said, "I guess…"

"I believe it's worth fighting for. You can't let us down."

"Well, uh…"

"Tom?"

Tom was back with us. The Three Musketeers once more.

There's charisma for you.

FOURTEEN

APRIL 16

Sunday afternoon brought a thin spring rain, the kind that came down like a mist and kept you indoors when you would rather be outside. Lisa had been busy all morning, painting with her watercolors and playing with Pumpkin, but now, just as I was about to join the boys for a meeting, she wanted me to play Scrabble with her.

"How come you're always having meetings with the guys in their room? What are the meetings about? Why don't you ever let me come?" She twisted a lock of her dark hair into a ringlet and blinked at me from behind her glasses.

"I'll try not to be too long. We'll play Scrabble later, okay?" I grabbed my math book.

They were waiting for me, Billy lounging on his bed and Tom working on a Sudoku puzzle on the floor. The window was open a few inches, and I could hear the whoosh and clatter of a SkyTrain on the tracks below. The noise never bothered the boys. They always slept through it. So they said.

After our last bank disaster, Billy had come up with a new idea.

That was what the meeting was all about.

"It's a new MO," he said and then waited for us to digest this information.

Billy likes fancy crime words. MO means *modus operandi*, he'd explained to us, which is police language for method of operation. Billy said that criminals usually stuck with the same MO when they committed crimes, and only ever changed their MO when it stopped working for them.

"Why do we need a new MO?" asked Tom. "Because you were caught in the drugstore?"

Billy shook his head, smiling at Tom. "As I've said before, being caught is not important when they don't find the loot on you. No loot, no case. No, what I'm getting at is the miserable take last time. A measly hundred and fifty bucks. Not good enough. It'll take us years to reach our goal at this rate."

That's exactly what I'd been thinking. "So what's your plan, Billy?" I asked.

Billy relaxed into his usual pose, lounging back against his headboard, hands behind his head, eyes swiveling from Tom, up to the ceiling and down to me on the beanbag near the door.

Tom put down his Sudoku and cracked his knuckles.

Billy flinched.

"So what's the plan?" Tom asked.

"We hit harder. Instead of robbing from just one teller we rob from all of them."

Tom and I were stunned into silence.

Tom was the first to speak. "And how do you propose to do that?"

"Simple. This is how I see it shaking down. Tom, you're still our handoff man. You wait in your usual spot down the street. But this time Nails and I go in together a few minutes before closing time. She's got a disguise too. As soon as we're in disguise we go into action. I yell for the tellers to put all their money on the counter. I pretend I've got a gun. Nell goes along the counter with her shopping bag and scoops up all the loot. Then we both run for it. The cash and disguises go into Tom's backpack. We all separate. SkyTrain escape as usual."

Silence. My heart went numb. I would have to go right in there, into the bank, and scoop up the money.

"Won't work," Tom said after a while.

Billy's eyebrows shot up one sixty-fourth of a centimeter. "Why not?"

"I dunno. It just seems crazy. Way riskier too, with more people in the bank knowing there's a robbery happening. Before, only the one teller knew it was a robbery. With this new idea there's way more chance of being caught. And I don't like the idea of a gun."

Billy blinked. "But there won't *be* a gun."

Crack-crack. "I know, but I don't even like the idea of a pretend gun."

Billy looked over at me. "What do you think, Nails?"

It was hard to think with a numb heart. "It could work, I guess," I said after a few seconds.

Billy smiled.

I was astonished. Those words came out of my mouth? What was happening to me? Was I catching Billy's buccaneer fever? Was I becoming addicted to excitement? Was it because I would do anything for us to stay together? Or was I just trying to please Billy?

I thought I knew the answer. I said quickly, "But I agree with Tom."

Billy's smile disappeared. "You do?"

"Tom's right. It's too risky. We could get caught. And I don't like the idea of a gun either, even if it's not real. What if someone in the bank has a gun and they think we have guns? Wouldn't they shoot us? If we're disguised, they won't know we're just kids. They would just shoot us, thinking I'm a disguised dwarf. Besides, I couldn't do a thing like that, scooping up the money. I'd have a heart attack."

Billy shrugged, disappointed. "Okay, forget about it."

I hated letting him down.

Tom said, "I've got a suggestion for improving our getaway. It's the handoffs. I think I should be waiting round a corner instead of on the same street as the bank."

Billy mumbled, "Oh yeah?"

Tom said to Billy, "Right now, if someone sees you put the money and disguise in Nails' shopping bag, they will watch where she goes and then see me. The whole idea of having a second handoff is so that won't happen."

"So what do you suggest?" Billy asked.

"That I be hidden from sight around the corner from the bank. Nails leaves the bank, walks to the end of the block, turns the corner, makes the handoff. Anyone watching from the bank won't see anything."

"Good idea, Tom," said Billy. "Nails?"

I thought for a second or two. "I like it, but it still doesn't solve the problem of taking big risks for small amounts of money."

"I say we carry on," said Billy. "Small amounts will add up to big amounts. We've just gotta keep going."

"We've made almost three thousand so far," said Tom. "That's an average of almost a thousand dollars on each holdup."

I shook my head. "You're wrong, Tom. If you count the holdup where the teller screamed, and we got a big fat zero, the average is only about—what?"

"Okay, you're right, Nails. That would make it seven hundred for each holdup." Tom nodded. "I forgot we did four."

"All the more reason to try my new MO," argued Billy. "Our average would skyrocket if we robbed two or three tellers at the same time."

"Count me out," said Tom.

"Me too," I said. "Too risky. Holdups number one and three were good, over twenty-five hundred total." I had the numbers memorized. "I say let's continue as we are. No changes. No new MO. Just Tom's idea, the change in the handoff."

"Agreed," said Tom.

Billy shrugged. "Okay."

FIFTEEN

We chose our next bank by studying the phone book and a street map.

It would be a small Bank of Hong Kong in Vancouver's Eastside. Billy planned the holdup for Thursday the twentieth. He thought that ten minutes before three o'clock would be a good time. We skipped out of school an hour early on Monday and took the SkyTrain to check everything out. We checked the bank, front and back. We checked the layout inside. We decided where the handoffs would be made— Tom around the corner this time, away from the bank sightlines, and me right outside the bank entrance, as usual.

It was a nice little bank.

The SkyTrain station was only two blocks away.

"It's going to be a real pleasure knocking this one over," said Billy.

He was getting more and more professional.

And charismatic.

$ $ $

Billy and I headed into the bank about ten minutes before closing time and lingered at a desk, pretending to be busy. The bank seemed larger than it was because it was all glass and light. Even on a dull rainy day like this one, the interior was bright and spacious.

Billy wore his usual disguise.

It was a cold day, but I was sweating.

There were only two customers with tellers and an old guy looking through brochures near the manager's office. The manager's office door was closed, which was the way we liked it. We didn't want a manager peeping out to see what was going on.

Billy walked up to the teller—she looked like a high school kid, not much older than me, small, lots of makeup, blond curls. I left the bank and stood outside.

I waited for a while and then I knew something had gone wrong. Billy should have been out at least a minute ago. I pushed open the door and looked inside. Billy was wrestling with the man who had been reading brochures. He didn't look so old now. He clamped onto Billy's arm like a vulture.

Just as some of the other bank workers started running over to help the man, Billy shook himself free, and erupted through the door. We ran together down the street. I handed him my shopping bag. Billy stuffed his disguise and the loot in the bag and shoved it back at me. Sweating and breathing heavily, he crossed the street and disappeared down a narrow lane.

Wondering if anyone had seen me, I continued to the end of the block, whispering to myself, "Stay calm. Stay calm." I turned the corner, and made my handoff to Tom. Without a word, Tom crammed my bag into his backpack, casually crossed the street and followed Billy to the station. I walked back to the corner and looked toward the bank. Everything, except my heart, was quiet. Then I heard a police siren, and I was out of there.

$ $ $

I collapsed onto the beanbag. "That was close, Billy."

Tom threw himself onto his bed. "Too friggin' close, if you ask me. Who was the guy who jumped you—a security guard?"

Billy sighed and lowered himself slowly onto his bed and assumed his usual position. "No. Don't think so. He was just a madman who happened to be there. Maybe he saw the teller crying, put two and two together and jumped me."

"The teller was crying?" Tom's eyes widened in disbelief.

Billy was subdued. There was none of his usual devil-may-care attitude.

He said, "I think that's what she was doing. I saw tears. But she didn't make any noise. As a matter of fact, she was real quiet."

Tom and I digested this disturbing information in silence.

"Poor kid," I said.

Tom said, "I don't like this. I never did. It's a dirty business. We're messing with people's lives."

I didn't say anything, but I thought Tom was right. It was a dirty business. It was cruel to cause someone pain.

Billy said, "That bank had drop boxes. I saw them."

This was new to me. "What's a drop box?"

Billy leaned his head back and looked up at the ceiling. "Each teller has a drop box. When the drawer starts filling up with bills they're supposed to drop them through a slot in their desk into a security box—a kind of miniature vault—under the counter. They don't have a key to get into it."

"Oh yeah," said Tom. "So what's that got to do with the girl crying?"

Billy said gloomily. "Take a look in your backpack and maybe you'll figure it out."

We had completely forgotten about the money. Tom picked up his backpack, pulled out my shopping bag and emptied it onto his bed.

Bills, bills and more bills—more than we'd ever seen.

Tom was speechless.

I was flabbergasted.

I looked at Billy's gloomy face, and I wondered why the sudden change of mood, especially since the robbery appeared to have been such a winner. "What are you saying, Billy? That the girl hadn't got rid of her overstocked bills? Bills she should have sent to the drop box? And that's why she was crying? Not because she was scared?"

"That's the way I see it," Billy said wearily.

Now I understood. He felt sorry for the girl.

"She'll be sacked," I said. "That's terrible."

Billy looked even gloomier. "Yeah. Too bad for her…" He brightened a little. "But good for us."

We counted the money. But our hearts were not in it.

The total was $2,750.

It was the most we had ever made in one hit.

We were more than halfway to our goal.

But we didn't celebrate. We were still thinking of the girl's tears.

"We should give it back," growled Tom, "and ask them not to fire the girl. Everyone makes mistakes. 'Even monkeys fall from trees,' my dad used to say whenever I messed up."

Billy and I knew that giving back the money was not a practical solution, so we said nothing. Besides, the money brought us that much closer to the ten thousand we needed.

Tom started pacing the room. "Surely, there's *something* we can do," he said.

Tom was often a big pain in the butt—like grabbing the bathroom when it wasn't his turn, and complaining about my ball-passing and my spaghetti-eating—but of the three of us, he had the softest heart.

SIXTEEN

The next day I was pulling on my raincoat, about to leave for school, when Janice stopped me.

"Nell, before you go, I want to talk to you."

She was serious. I tensed. Had she found out something?

"It's about Billy," she said.

"Yes?" I said cautiously.

Maybe she'd overheard our meetings. Maybe Lisa had heard something and had told her.

"It's his birthday today."

"Billy's? Oh, I didn't know that."

"And I want to give him a little surprise tonight. His favorite supper, lasagna, and a big cake with strawberries."

I smiled. "He'll like that."

"I tried telling Tom this morning, but I couldn't get him alone. And the guys have already left. Could you ask Tom to keep Billy busy for an hour or so after school? They could go to the park and play basketball or something. Give us time to get supper all ready."

"Sure. I could do that."

"But don't tell Billy. I want it to be a surprise. And here's five dollars. Maybe you could buy him a little treat. He loves those Cadbury Fruit and Nut bars. Maybe you could get him a giant one at the drugstore. Now you better get going, you're late."

The first bell had already rung by the time I got to school. The corridors were empty, so I didn't see Tom. He wasn't in any of my classes, so I'd have to grab him at lunch. I didn't usually talk to Tom at school. We swung in different circles.

At lunchtime I found him in the cafeteria, surrounded by fellow geeks. I brushed past him with my tray of soup and crackers.

"Got to talk to you," I told him on my way to a table where Liesel would join me.

Tom followed me.

"What's up?"

I scanned the cafeteria and spotted Billy in the food lineup. "It's Billy," I said. "It's his birthday today, and Janice wants to give him a surprise supper. Can you meet him after school and go to the mall or play basketball or something for an hour while we get stuff ready?"

"Sure, no problem."

After school the sun was dodging in and out of fluffy white clouds—a rare event. I was about to head over to Go Rite Drugs to buy Billy's chocolate bar when I thought maybe I could get him something from my favorite store, Value Village. It wasn't much farther away.

The clouds were reflected in the puddles. Shafts of sunshine shot down through the trees. Raindrops glistened on new green leaves. I felt good as I moved with purpose along the street.

There was always a musty crusty smell in Value Village, probably from the tons of unwashed clothes people donated. They were supposed to be cleaned, but I doubted it. The lighting, always on the dim side, was bright enough for me to see that the store was crowded. There were lots of oldies and several teens, but I didn't recognize anyone from school.

Billy was not much into clothes, but I plowed through rows of wrinkled shirts and dusty pants in the men's section. At the end of the rack of coats, I spotted a black leather jacket. My heart skipped. Maybe this was it, I told myself, slipping it off the hanger. The jacket was heavy. Must be the real thing, I thought, genuine leather.

I pulled it on over my raincoat. The leather was butter soft and enfolded me in a sweet leathery smell. It hung halfway to my knees. The sleeves dangled several inches past my hands. I thought it would fit Billy just fine. I smiled, thinking how cool he would look in it, like James Dean from the biker movies. Every time he wore it, he would think, "Yes. I got this cool jacket from Nails."

I pulled out the price tag: $17.00. My heart sank. I'd already checked my wallet. Counting the $5.00 from Janice, I had $12.63. That was my total wealth.

I looked around. No one was watching me. I could just walk out the front door. No one would notice. Heck, I just robbed a bunch of banks. Stealing a jacket would be child's play.

I started moving down the row of racks, swishing past the musty clothes. There was a mirror at the end of the row. I stopped and looked at the shine of the leather in the reflection. I pushed the hair away from my face. In this light my hair looked almost black too. It was long enough to pull into a ponytail, but today I had left it loose.

"Yes." I nodded to my pale face in the mirror. "This jacket is perfect for Billy. I've got to have it." The Nails in the mirror nodded agreeably.

There was a sign beside the cashier: *Value Village profits go to a worthy cause. Thanks for your generosity*.

One of the cashiers, an older Asian woman, looked up and smiled at me, nodding slightly in the way some Asian people have, showing respect, I guess.

"Um," I said before I even realized I was doing it, "could you keep this jacket for me? I'm just going home to get a bit more money."

"We keep items just one hour," she said, looking regretful. "That okay?"

"Yes." I nodded.

"What name?"

"Name? Oh, it's Nell."

I knew exactly where I could get the extra cash.

When I got home, Janice was cooking. Spicy smells of oregano and tomato wafted up from the sauce simmering on the stove.

"Nell? Is that you?" she called from the kitchen.

"Hi, Janice," I said at the kitchen door.

"Just have to finish beating up these egg whites. Cake should be ready in about an hour. Did you tell Tom about tonight?"

"Yes. Look, I have to go out again to get Billy's present. But I'll be back in plenty of time to give you a hand."

I headed upstairs to my bedroom—and the stash under the floorboards. I'd grab just a few dollars. It was for a worthy cause, I told myself, a very worthy cause.

But once I was in the bedroom, I couldn't do it. I couldn't take the money out of the box. That money was for a new bathroom so the four of us kids could stay here. It was not for anything else. Spending the money on other stuff would make the bank robberies wrong somehow.

Lisa came into the room.

"Hi, Nell," she said. "I'm making a birthday card for Billy. A caterpillar changing into a butterfly. What do you think?"

"Cute. A birthday butterfly. Good idea. He'll like it."

"Do you want to sign it?"

"Sure." I rummaged through my desk for a pen. "Say, Lisa. Do you have any cash?"

"Not much. Maybe five or six dollars in my froggy bank."

I told her about the jacket and how I needed just five dollars more to buy it. "Then it could be from both of us," I told her.

The Asian woman wasn't at the cash register when I got there. And there was no sign of the jacket at her counter. I panicked.

"You were holding a black leather jacket for me," I told the cashier, a thin young woman wearing so much mascara she looked like a raccoon.

"We can keep items for only an hour," she said with a shrug.

Then I spotted the jacket hanging on a rack waiting to be returned to the shopping area. I grabbed it and breathed in the leathery smell. I smiled to myself. Perfect.

The cashier folded the jacket and stuffed it into a big paper grocery bag.

When I got home, Janice called from the kitchen, "Nell? Is that you?"

"Yes, I'm home," I told her as I shucked off my raincoat.

"Good. Can you come and give me a hand?"

Lisa was in the kitchen as well, mixing juice. "Did you get it?" she asked.

"Yes." I smiled at her. "He'll love it. Want to put the card inside?"

She did and I put the bag on Billy's chair.

"What did you get?" Janice asked. "Sure doesn't look like a chocolate bar to me."

Before I could tell her, the guys bounced in. Janice hurried them out of the kitchen. "Can't come in yet," she told them. "We're not quite ready."

"What's going on?" Billy asked. "First, Tom insists on playing basketball for more than an hour. And now we can't come into the kitchen?"

"Come on, Billy. Maybe we can get our homework started." Tom pushed him toward the stairs.

"But I'm starving," Billy complained. "And whatever's cooking in there smells so great. Can't we at least get a snack?"

"Supper in twenty minutes," Janice said. "Tops. Go up to your room and we'll call you down as soon as we're ready."

After the boys went upstairs, I made the salad and set the table.

Joseph came home soon after.

"We're almost ready," Janice told him as she kissed him hello. "Want to call the guys?"

"Surprise!" we all yelled as the boys entered the kitchen.

"Happy birthday, Billy," said Janice.

Billy's usually sleepy eyes widened and his eyebrows shot up. He raked his hair away from his face and grinned. "For me?" he said. "I didn't think anyone would remember my birthday."

"How could we forget one of our favorite kids in the whole world," Janice said, giving him a hug. "Happy fifteenth, dear."

Joseph shook his hand solemnly, then grabbed him in a jolly bear hug. "Happy birthday, big guy." He handed him a small package wrapped in shiny green paper. "This is from Janice and me."

Billy ripped off the wrapping. "Cool!" he said. "A digital watch! Thanks a lot."

"It's got an alarm," Janice told him. "So no more excuses for being late or sleeping in."

Lisa pushed me forward. I got the bag from the chair. "This is from Lisa and me."

It was bizarre how shy I was feeling. He'd probably hate the jacket. He'd think it was just some grungy old thing.

Billy looked into the bag and pulled out the card. "Did you paint this yourself?" he asked Lisa.

"Of course!" She laughed, excited.

"Cool," he said, grinning at her. "Thanks." He bent and kissed her on the cheek.

Then he emptied the bag onto his chair. He took a step back like he was in shock. "No way!" he breathed. "No fantastical way!" He pulled on the jacket, and, as I had thought, it fitted him perfectly. He zipped it up and put a hand into one of the pockets. He shook his head and stroked the front, and for a moment he seemed to be in a daze. Then he said in a quiet voice, "My dad. He had a jacket just like this one. Same kind of pockets. Same smell. A big giant guy, he was. Rode a motorcycle. He used to give me rides around the block when I was real small. Haven't seen him since he…" His voice trailed off.

Silence.

"Hey, guys. Lasagna's growing cold," Janice said quickly. "Let's eat."

Billy nodded and looked at me. Seemed to me his eyes were a little damp. "Thanks, Nell," he said. His voice was husky. "Thanks a lot." He turned to Lisa. "Thanks, Princess."

It was a lovely birthday supper.

SEVENTEEN

APRIL 25

Less than a week later, I was standing with Billy outside the Canadian Imperial Bank on Broadway. Tom was in position around the corner on Commercial Drive.

It was raining—as usual.

When we had cased the bank a few days ago, I saw that there was no place out of the rain, so I had borrowed an umbrella from Janice when I left for school. Billy and I were sheltered under it as we waited.

If I looked up, I could see the elevated SkyTrain track over Ninth Avenue. Broadway Station was only yards away. Tucked under my left arm was my brown shopping bag, handles to the top.

Billy watched the bank, waiting for a good time to go in. The street was busy with people coming and going to the SkyTrain station or shopping along Broadway. A panhandler on the other side of the street, filthy red scarf knotted around his neck, sat on the step outside Shoppers Drug Mart, oblivious to the rain. An old woman stopped and asked Billy something. I couldn't hear over the traffic noises. She leaned her umbrella out of the way so as not to poke him in the eye. Billy pointed toward the train station and said something to the woman. She nodded and moved away.

We waited a while longer, and then Billy leaned toward me and said, "It's time," and headed into the bank.

I waited, shifting from one foot to the other. It was a cold day, but I was starting to sweat as usual inside my raincoat.

A bus roared by and I suddenly felt my shopping bag being ripped from under my arm as the rain-soaked panhandler, the guy with the red scarf— I hadn't seen him cross the street—ran off with my bag in his hand.

Thief! Bag snatcher!

But I couldn't yell. Attracting attention would mean disaster, the end of everything.

The panhandler probably thought my empty bag was a purse. But now what? I didn't have anything for the handoff. As I was wondering what to do, Billy exploded through the glass door of the bank and I moved with him. I pulled my umbrella half-closed and pointed it down to the ground. Billy, quick to understand, dropped everything into the umbrella. I clamped it shut. Billy took off into the train station. I hurried around the corner and made a handoff to Tom by emptying the contents of the umbrella into his backpack. He disappeared.

I tucked the umbrella under my arm and headed for the corner to cross Commercial Drive. A hand on my shoulder pulled me back and my heart stopped.

"Hold it, kid! Show me that umbrella of yours."

I was too stunned to move. A man grabbed the umbrella, turned it over and shook it with one hand while he kept a grip on my upper arm with the other.

My arm and shoulder hurt.

He was dressed in a dark suit and wore a tie. His face was wet from the rain. I knew he was from the bank and that he must have seen Billy make his handoff into my umbrella.

When he found nothing he looked puzzled. He hurled the umbrella to the ground, grabbed my shoulders and shook me with both hands. "Where's the money, you little crook? What did you do with it?"

My teeth rattled. I couldn't speak.

"Thief!" he yelled in my ear. "Dirty little brat. Where is it?"

"No!" I yelled. His fingers were steel claws biting into my arms. I tried to pull away from him, but his grip was unyielding. "Not me."

"Liar! I saw you! Outside the bank. I saw you... Scum! That's what you are—thieving scum!"

"You're crazy! Let me go! You're hurting me. I don't know anything. You got me mixed up with someone else. Ouch! Let go of me! Help!" I yelled loud as I could. "Help!"

People were staring.

I screamed at him, "You're hurting me!"

He darted a glance at the onlookers. A shadow of uncertainty flashed across his face. His grip loosened. I spun away quickly and lashed out with my right foot, nailing him on the shin—bull's-eye. I followed it up with a fast kick to his other shin.

"Aaargh!" he screamed, hopping about in pain.

I charged into him like a linebacker, shoulder forward, and he fell to the pavement. Then I grabbed Janice's umbrella and zipped across the street, less than ten feet in front of a bus—I could hear the astonished squeal of brakes. I didn't look back. I dashed into the SkyTrain station and hurled myself up the escalator. I was lucky—a train was just pulling in. Panting, I mingled with the people boarding the train. I looked behind me. Nobody was after me. The bell gave its three-tone ring and the doors closed with a hiss.

Trembling and breathless, I collapsed into an empty seat and doubled over. My arms hurt. My stomach churned.

The train surged forward.

I was safe.

I had almost been caught, almost handed over to the police.

I was terrified.

$ $ $

"What happened?"

Billy and Tom were waiting for me.

"You look like you've been crying," said Tom, cracking his knuckles furiously.

I was so upset that I wasn't able to sit on the beanbag, so I paced the room as I told my story.

"Please stop with that," Billy said to Tom when I had finished.

"What?"

"The bones."

"Sorry."

"Were you really crying?" asked Billy. "Or were you faking it?"

"Crying? Me? No way. But I'll admit I was scared all right. I was sure I was about to be hauled off to jail."

"Nails, you had nothing on you but a harmless umbrella," said Billy. "There was nothing to connect you with the robbery."

"Except a witness," said Tom.

"Unreliable," said Billy. "He had no proof. What happened to your shopping bag anyway?"

I told him.

"A series of unfortunate events," Tom said. "How much did we make?" he asked Billy.

Billy reached underneath his pillow and tossed the money onto the bed.

I counted it: $350. All that stress and aggravation for a mere $350? I threw it back onto the bed. Nobody said anything.

A SkyTrain clattered by underneath the window.

EIGHTEEN

APRIL 28

A few days had gone by since our last holdup, and Billy had said nothing about our next one. Not a word. It was like he'd suddenly forgotten about our sacred mission. He acted strange the rest of the week, going around with a long face and talking to hardly anyone. He got home from school late every day, making it just in time for supper. If it wasn't his turn on kitchen duty, he headed straight up to his room after dinner.

Janice knew something, but she wasn't letting on.

$ $ $

"What's up with the big guy?" Tom asked me on the bus Friday morning. Billy was sitting up front, plugged into his earphones and staring out the window.

I shrugged. "I don't know. Maybe he's sick or something."

"I don't think he's sick. But he lies in bed every night staring at the ceiling, not saying anything. You should talk to him, Nails. Find out what's going on. Maybe we can help him."

I didn't get a chance to talk to Billy, but when I got out of my last class the next day, Billy was waiting for me in the hall. "I need you to come somewhere with me, okay?"

I grabbed my coat out of my locker and followed him.

"Where are we going?"

He had his hands shoved deep into his pockets and he was looking straight ahead. He mumbled something, but a truck splashed by and I couldn't hear what he said.

"Where did you say?"

"Hospital."

"Why? You sick or something?"

"'Course not. They said I could bring someone, a friend."

"They? Who? Billy, tell me why we're going to the hospital."

He looked down at me. "It's my dad," he said, louder.

"Your dad? You've got a dad?"

Just a week ago, Billy said he hadn't seen his dad in a long time, so I figured he was probably dead. His mom had disappeared a few years ago—never came back from visiting a friend. She just vanished without a trace.

By now we had reached the SkyTrain station. We slid our passes into the slot, and I followed him into the crowd standing near the tracks waiting for the westbound train.

"So what's this about your dad?" I asked him.

"He's…"

The train arrived and the doors slid open. We pushed inside with the rest of the crowd. Then we were separated by two old women gabbing in loud voices.

"…thinks I should get a tint," shouted one old woman with puffy grey hair. "Put in some red high-lights, she said. I'll look stylish, she said."

"Oh no! Don't do it." The other old crone shook her head. She was wearing a wooly tea-cozy for a hat. "She's just after your money. Besides, once you start coloring your hair, you have to keep on doing it, you know. The expense. Oh, the terrible expense."

Billy stood, hanging on to the rail. I moved quickly into a vacant seat beside a woman with long dark hair. It was no use trying to talk to Billy here.

We got to Joyce Street Station and the dark-haired woman got off. I stood while Billy slid in next to the window. Then I sat beside him.

"Tell me about your dad."

He shook his head. "Later." He turned away and looked out the window.

When we stopped at Broadway Station, Billy didn't move. So I knew we weren't going to Vancouver General Hospital.

At Burrard Street Station, Billy sat and looked out at the platform. A bunch of giggling teens made their way to the escalator. This was the stop for St. Paul's Hospital. We had run out of hospitals.

"Shouldn't we be getting off?" I asked him.

He shook his head.

There was only one more stop, and I was beginning to think I hadn't heard Billy right. Maybe he'd said hostel, not hospital. But what about Lions Gate Hospital on the North Shore? Maybe we were heading for the SeaBus.

We were at the end of the line, Waterfront Station. I followed Billy off the train, up the escalator and out onto Cordova Street. So it wasn't to be Lions Gate. Billy steered me east through the rain toward Gastown. He didn't say a word. I was beginning to worry. Had he lost it? Had his mind suddenly flipped? We left Gastown behind and marched along Water Street onto Powell. Everyone walked past a man lying unconscious in a shop doorway, cradling a wine bottle in his arms. This was the downtown eastside where the drunks and the drug addicts and the homeless people hung out. Well, we were criminals now. We belonged here.

$ $ $

We came to a small brick building with a sign planted in the scruffy grass: *May's Place* in big letters, and underneath that, *The May Gutteridge Community Home.*

"Come on," Billy said, leading the way through the door. He stopped at a small reception desk, and an older woman with white hair and a nurse's uniform flashed him a saintly smile. "Hello, Billy," she said. "Hang your coats on the rack and go right up."

I followed Billy up a flight of stairs and down a hall. This had to be the smallest hospital in the world. The doors were open. I counted six beds, one per room, all occupied. I turned my eyes away, trying not to stare. Billy had obviously been here before. He stopped in front of an open door, and we went in. The small room smelled of disinfectant. The walls were painted a light blue. A window looked out at another building. In the bed was a geezer with his eyes closed. He looked like he might be dead. Then I remembered why we were here. This geezer was Billy's dad.

Billy pulled two chairs over to the bed, one on each side, and sat in the one close to the window. I sat, wondering what I was doing here. I hated hospitals.

The room was silent.

"Funny little hospital," I whispered.

Billy looked at me from the other side of his dad's bed. "It's a hospice."

"A hospice?"

"For the downtown eastside people."

Then I remembered that a hospice is a place where people go to die.

Billy said, "He's got cancer real bad. The doctor told me it's only a matter of days."

I had never been in a room with a dying person before. It was a bit scary. I imagined Death dressed in black, hovering over the bed like a filmy ghost, waiting to take Billy's dad away.

I looked at the frail old man's face. He looked pinched and pale and had thin bloodless lips. I saw no resemblance to Billy whatsoever.

"Your dad lived around here?"

"Yeah. I just found out. Few days ago. He's been here three weeks. Social Services called Janice. My old man had put me down as his next of kin."

On his birthday, Billy said that his dad had been a big guy who wore a leather jacket like the one I gave him. Maybe the man sleeping in the bed had been big once, but he wasn't big now. "Was that the last time you saw him, when you were little and he gave you rides on his motorcycle?"

Billy nodded. "One day he went off on his motorcycle, and I never saw him again."

A nurse with short black hair came in, smiled at us, looked at the sleeping man, took his pulse and left.

We sat in silence for a long time. Billy's dad didn't wake up.

I got pins and needles in my legs.

Billy sighed. Then he leaned toward the bed. "We better be going, Dad," he said in the old man's ear.

His dad didn't move. His faint breathing was barely detectable.

We left.

Walking back to Waterfront Station in the rain, I said, "Why did you want me to come with you, Billy?"

"I dunno. It helps." He shrugged awkwardly. "When he's awake he never talks, just looks at me. Or he turns his head away and looks at the wall. One day I was there and he cried. I ask him things, but he never answers, never says anything. Just looks at me. I thought if you were there he might say something. A pretty girl in the room might make him talk, you know?"

I didn't say anything. I felt like crying.

$ $ $

We went again the next morning, not talking much during the forty-minute trip. The SkyTrain was quiet, even for a Saturday. I'd never seen Billy so down.

The same nurse was at the desk. "Doctor Watterson just left, Billy. Your father is sleeping comfortably."

We sat down and waited to see if he'd wake up. The room was brighter than yesterday. We didn't whisper this time but talked in our normal voices.

"Have you talked with this Dr. Watterson?"

Billy nodded.

"Does he know anything about your dad's life—before he came here?"

"He was a regular customer at Mental Health Services where Dr. Watterson works. My dad's an alcoholic. But he had friends. He tried to help other people like himself. And Dr. Watterson tried to help him."

I got an eerie feeling someone else was in the room, and then I noticed that Billy's dad was awake. He stared at Billy with bright blue eyes. There was no mistaking those eyes. He suddenly looked like Billy.

"Hi, Dad," Billy said quietly.

His dad continued to stare but said nothing. Then his eyes switched to me like a question mark.

"This is my friend, Nails. She's in my foster. Her real name is Nell."

The old man tried to speak. The effort caused his thin chest to heave and his brow to wrinkle like corrugated cardboard. He managed to whisper, "Nell."

I smiled. "Hi."

His eyes turned to his son. "Billy," he croaked. He tried to say more but couldn't. He closed his eyes and sank back into his pillow.

Billy talked to him, but there was no response.

He was asleep again.

I asked Billy, "Was it weird seeing him here like this after all these years? Aren't you mad at him for leaving you?"

Billy's eyes widened. "Mad? No, I don't think so. Not mad. I feel sorry for him, that's all, for wasting his life."

"What about what he did to your life?"

He shrugged. "I didn't have a dad when I needed one. He did that to me. Maybe I should be mad, but I'm not. He was weak, that's all. I won't ever be weak like him. I've promised myself that."

The nurse at the desk downstairs beamed one of her saintly smiles at us as we left.

$ $ $

By now, Tom knew the cause of Billy's troubles.

"Want to come with us, Tom?" said Billy on Sunday afternoon.

"Okay," said Tom. "If you're sure you want me to come."

This time when we got to the hospice, the doctor and nurse were in the room with Billy's dad, so we had to wait. When they came out, the doctor said, "I've given him something to make him comfortable, Billy."

The doctor seemed nice. He was wearing a gray tracksuit and running shoes.

We all went in and sat. The old man's eyes were closed. His breath came in quick raspy puffs. He opened his eyes and looked at Billy, and without moving his head he looked at me. Then his eyes went back to his son. He didn't seem to notice Tom. He tried to speak, but all that came out was a grunt. He slowly reached a frail hand out to Billy. Billy clasped his father's hand in his own big fist and moved closer.

His dad made a single powerful effort to speak. "Billy?"

Billy stared into his father's eyes. "What is it, Dad?"

The old man gathered a second breath. "I'm... sorry...Billy."

Billy wrapped his arms around his father and hugged him to his chest. He spoke a few words into his dad's ear. Then he laid him gently back onto the pillow.

I couldn't hear what Billy said because of his father's rattling breath.

The old man's eyes closed, and in a second he was asleep, the wrinkles gone and the beginning of a smile on his thin lips.

Billy decided to stay, so Tom and I made our way home, mainly in silence. Tom stared out the SkyTrain window. When we we got to Patterson and stood by the door, waiting to get off, I caught a glimpse of Tom's eyes. They were damp and pink, like he'd been crying. He'd been thinking about Billy's dad, I guessed. Or remembering his own dad—his lost family.

$ $ $

Billy stayed at the hospice all night and came home the next morning while we were eating breakfast. His face was white. He looked beat.

Janice jumped up from the table to meet him. "How is he, Billy?"

Billy said nothing and stood looking at Janice helplessly.

We all knew.

Janice flung her arms around Billy. Joseph stood and put his arms around Billy's and Janice's shoulders. Tom, Lisa and I joined the group, looping our arms around each other in a family hug.

NINETEEN

MAY 4

We skipped out of school early again and rode the SkyTrain to the big city.

The Three Musketeers.

I had a bad feeling about this holdup.

We were socked in with the usual West Coast—"wet" coast—rain and a cold wind that went right through my wet raincoat and chilled my bones. I was probably getting the flu or mad cow disease or something equally terrible. I had a crushing headache and my nose was running.

We took our positions: Billy outside the Vancity Savings Bank, me close by and Tom out of sight around the corner.

This was our seventh bank robbery. Wasn't seven supposed to be an unlucky number?

I sniffed and searched my pockets for a tissue. I had none. I wiped my nose on my jacket sleeve like a little kid. The waterproof fabric rejected the mucus, leaving the smear on my face.

From my lookout under the Shoe Warehouse awning, I could see the bank was busy. Maybe Billy's planning wasn't as good as he thought. Or maybe he chose a busy bank day deliberately to raise the bar on his excitement index.

A guy was hanging out in a beige Honda across the street. He sat behind the wheel, sipping coffee from a plastic cup and watching people going in and out of the shops. He looked across at Billy.

Was he a detective? Had the police finally caught up with us?

The man stared at me. Maybe he wasn't a cop. Maybe he was looking to pick up a street kid. I knew that happened to kids: guys pretending to ask for directions end up offering money for sex.

Sicko.

I jammed my fists into my pockets and turned my back on the guy.

I checked my watch. It was 1:22 PM.

Billy was taking forever. What was going on in that bank? He should have called off the holdup if it was too dangerous.

The freaky guy in the Honda drove away. That was a relief. I wiped my nose on my sleeve again.

Finally, at 1:26 PM, Billy gave the signal and I headed over to the bank.

Billy presented his note, and as the terrified teller was reaching into the drawer for the cash, I left to wait outside.

Billy came flying out of the bank, flipped off his ballcap, mustache and glasses, and dropped them into my bag along with the money. Then he took off around the corner, heading for the mall.

I moved down the street in the other direction, turned the corner and made the handoff to Tom. Tom grabbed my bag and disappeared.

It was 1:32 PM.

I walked back toward the bank, muttering, "Be calm. Be calm."

Out of the corner of my eye, I saw that the beige Honda was back.

The driver was watching me. It was creeping me out.

Was this it? Was I was about to be arrested? Thank God I didn't have the money. Had the Honda creep seen the handoffs?

"Hey! Girl!" He pulled up beside me.

He looked like an undercover cop sure enough. He needed a shave, and he had a bald head, pock-marked face and wet lips.

"Hey, girl? Stop right there!"

I turned to face him, head and heart pounding, nose running like a tap. He was close. Too close.

He grinned, baring yellow teeth. "I been watchin' you."

I said nothing and stared at the wet lips.

"You're real pretty. You know that, girl? You wanna make fifty bucks?"

I spat a big gob of snot in his ugly face and bolted.

The SkyTrain station was less than a block away.

I ran as fast as I could. I took a quick look behind to see if the creep was following me, but I couldn't see him.

I was panting hard when I got to the SkyTrain station. I ducked inside and fed my pass into the slot. Then I jumped onto the train and dropped into the closest seat with a groan of relief.

There were only a few people in the carriage.

My nose was dripping. I was wet. I was cold. My head pounded.

The three-tone bell rang out, but before the doors could swish shut, someone jammed himself in between them and pushed his way inside.

The creep? I got ready to run to someone for help.

But it was only Tom.

"What are you doing here?" I hissed, glaring at him. "You're supposed to take a different train."

"Quit telling me what to do," he hissed back. He yanked the shopping bag out of his pack, flung it onto my lap and thumped down on the seat in front of me.

I grabbed the bag. "Look. The only way this will work is if we all do what we're supposed to. That's what Billy said. Okay?"

"I'm sick of it," he muttered. "I'm sick of you. And I'm sick of Billy."

"We'll get caught if we're not careful."

"So?"

"So if we're seen together someone might figure the whole thing out."

An old woman wearing a floppy rain hat turned and stared at us. Had she heard?

I shot her my mean squinty-eyed look. She turned away quickly to look out the gritty window.

"Anyway," I said, poking Tom's back. "You shouldn't be here."

"Look," Tom said. "Why should I stand out there in the rain, freezing my butt off, just because you said to?"

"It's all part of the plan. Surely even you can understand that?"

"Like I said, I'm sick of this whole deal. It's just not worth it."

"Not worth it? How can you say that? If we don't do this, you know we'll be sent away. They'll probably send you to someone like Mrs. Osberg, and she'll beat you with her cane. How will you like that?"

Tom shook his head. "Look," he said, keeping his voice low. "What we're doing is wrong. Wrong. Period. Besides, it just isn't working. There's no way we can get ten grand. Might as well be a million at the rate we're going." He cracked his knuckles. "I've had it. There's no way I'll let Billy talk me into it again." He made a fist with one hand and punched his other palm hard— again and again.

I flinched. I knew he was wishing it was Billy and me he was punching.

"You guys won't have me to boss around anymore," he growled.

He had quit for good this time. I could tell.

When we got to Patterson Station, I pushed through the crowd to get off quickly, but Tom was right behind me. He was out of the train and running down the escalator. I tried to get away so no one would know we were together. But he stuck to me like dog crap to the sole of a shoe. I swung the shopping bag ready to wallop him, but he stayed just out of my reach. I powered up the hill to the Hardy house. Tom was right behind me the whole time.

When we got to the front door, we were both breathless. He flicked his house key out of his pocket before I could dig out mine, unlocked the door and barged in ahead of me.

He stopped dead. I ran into him.

Uh-oh. Janice was here. She wasn't supposed to be home until four.

TWENTY

Janice poked her head out from the kitchen. "Hi there, you two. You're early. Want a cup of tea? I just made a fresh pot."

"Tea sounds good. Thanks," I said, trying to sound normal as I peeled off my soaked jacket and draped it over the rack by the front door. But what should I do with the bag? I couldn't leave it there.

Janice touched my forehead. "You're hot, Nell. And you look awful. A nice warm cup of tea and an aspirin is what you need. Then you should take a good long shower."

She disappeared into the kitchen. I followed reluctantly and grabbed a handful of tissues. Tom was right behind me. Janice gave us tea, scalding hot. "Did they let you out early today?"

I racked my brain for an explanation.

I started my lie. "The teachers let us out at noon because they have this very important meeting, so…"

Tom interrupted, puffing air out of his mouth like a blowfish. "That's a lie," he said flatly. He cracked his knuckles. "A total lie. We skipped out."

"Shut up," I hissed, glaring at him.

"Not only that," he went on, ignoring me, "we've been skipping out all month."

Janice said, "Skipping out of school? But…I don't get it." Her laugh was uncertain. "You're good kids, remember? Good kids don't skip out of school."

"Us? Good kids? Ha!" Tom laughed hoarsely. "That's a joke. You know what your good kids have been doing?" He turned his back on me. "We've been robbing banks."

My heart plunged. How could Tom be such a dirty traitor? After taking the oath of secrecy. I was horrified.

Janice's mouth dropped open. In a state of shock, she couldn't speak. Finally, she said, "Robbing…I don't understand."

"Show her the money, Nails," Tom demanded.

Janice turned to me, face collapsed like a burst basketball.

I clutched my shopping bag close and stood up.

Tom growled. "Come on. Let Janice see what's in the bag."

I backed away, clutching it to my chest.

Tom wrestled it from me and emptied it out onto the kitchen table. Billy's fake moustache, glasses and ballcap fell out. A few bills fluttered out of the cap.

"Go ahead, Janice," said Tom. "Take a look at what your good kids have done."

Janice picked up the bills. "You want to tell me where this money came from?" she asked me quietly.

I shrugged.

"From a bank in Vancouver," Tom told her. "Not much of a take this time though."

I was numb with shock.

"This time?" Janice said, her voice cracking. "You mean…"

There was a rattle at the front door and Billy came bumbling in, a grin plastered on his face. He noticed the shopping bag and its contents spread about the table. Then he looked at Janice holding the money. His grin vanished.

"Billy is in on this too," Tom told Janice. "We're bank robbers, all three of us."

Janice dropped the bills like they were suddenly red hot.

"I don't believe it!" she whispered.

"It's true," said Tom.

Janice stared at us, her eyes huge. I wished with all my being that I was somewhere else. Anywhere.

Janice made a visible effort to pull herself together.

"Take off your jacket and come and sit at the table," she told Billy in the voice she used when she wanted to sound tough. "And don't any of you move."

We sat. Billy stared at Tom, his brow furrowed like he was wondering what was going on. Tom wouldn't look at either of us.

It was turning into a nightmare. Tom was a dirty rotten fink, a traitor. He was our own Judas. Right then, I hated him.

Janice punched phone buttons.

Billy patted me lightly on the shoulder as if to say, "Don't worry."

How could I *not* worry when bombs were falling all around, when the earth was opening to swallow me up, when my whole life was sliding down the garbage chute?

Janice spoke into the phone. "Joseph. We've got a problem here. Can you come home? Nobody's injured, but we need you, okay?"

While we were waiting for Joseph, Janice started in with the questions. "Where is the rest of the money?"

I told her.

"Get it," she said.

Head pounding, I dragged myself up the stairs and got the shoe box from the closet. The running total on the lid was pitiful. A mere $5,470. We were only a little over halfway to our goal.

I took my time plodding down the stairs. Then I plunked the box on the table.

Janice looked inside, gasped, and then put the lid back on like it was full of deadly tarantulas.

By the time Joseph got home, Janice had a good idea of what had happened, so she explained it to him.

Joseph looked at Tom, then me and Billy, his kind face baffled, disappointed.

"Just how many banks did you rob?"

"Six," I said.

"Seven," said Billy, "if you include one failure."

Joseph's eyes popped. "Seven! How? How could three kids manage to rob seven banks and not get caught? I don't believe it!"

Tom told all.

Janice was struggling to hold back tears.

They listened. They didn't interrupt. When Tom had finished, Joseph asked, "But why? Why would you kids ever do such a crazy stupid thing?"

I said, "Because we don't want to leave here. Don't ever want to leave you and Janice."

Joseph frowned. "I don't get it."

"The money was for a new bathroom," I burst out. "We had no other choice."

Janice murmured faintly, "New bathroom?"

By now, what with my headache and running nose, and the horrible way I was feeling about disappointing Janice and Joseph, I couldn't stop the tears.

"That's why we needed ten grand," I cried. "We had this great system going. We would never get caught if Tom hadn't blabbed. We were going to get enough money to pay for the bathroom so none of us would have to leave."

Joseph shook his head. His voice rose. "Do you kids realize how dangerous it is to rob a bank?"

He got up from the table and started pacing, trying to control his anger. "You could be gunned down by security," he said. "You could be killed! And other people in the bank could be killed! For what? For a few lousy dollars?"

We all watched him. Nobody said a thing.

"Madness!" cried Joseph. "Were you on drugs?" He looked at me.

I shook my head. "No."

"We don't do drugs," said Billy. "You know that."

"I don't know anything," said Joseph. "Not after this, I don't!"

Janice said, "Take it easy, Joe."

Finally, he cooled down, stopped pacing and looked at each of us in turn—me, Billy, Tom—his face grim.

"You know what we've got to do, don't you?"

"What?" I said through my tissues and tears.

"Call the police, of course," said Joseph.

Tom's head snapped up. "Why can't you just punish us? We're just kids. We can't go to jail," he said.

"We've got no choice. Robbery is a crime, you know that. Crimes must be reported to the police. What did you think would happen?" Joseph asked him, amazed.

"I thought you'd just take the money and get the friggin' bathroom."

"We couldn't do that. It's stolen money. We could never use stolen money. Don't you see that?"

We sat there silent for a minute while the truth of what Joseph said sunk in.

Joseph gave a deep sigh. "You kids haven't thought this through very well, have you?" he said, reaching for the phone.

I dried my eyes with bunched tissues. "Wait," I said. "What if we turn ourselves in? What then?"

Joseph looked at Janice desperately.

"It would keep you and Janice out of it," I said to Joseph. "None of it is your fault."

"We don't want to be kept out of it," said Janice. "It is our fault. We knew something was going on, but we didn't know what. We should have asked more questions. I blame myself."

Joseph hung up the phone.

"I'm not turning myself in!" Tom said. "No friggin' way!"

Janice got up from the table and started filling the kettle. We all watched her in silence. She plugged in the kettle and then turned to face us. "Turn yourselves in or…"

We waited.

"Or we call the police." Joseph finished. "Now."

Head pounding, eyes watering, I said, "Don't worry, Janice. We'll do it."

Joseph said, "I'll drive you over there."

I looked at Billy. Billy put a hand on Tom's shoulder. Tom took a deep breath and then shrugged. "Okay," he said. "Let's do it."

"No," I said to Joseph. "You can trust us. We'll SkyTrain over."

I dragged myself upstairs to the shower.

TWENTY-ONE

I felt better after the hot shower and dry clothes. I emptied the money from the shoe box into the shopping bag and we SkyTrained downtown to the police station.

We were the Three Musketeers, together still, even though our secret was out, even though Tom had ratted us out.

It was funny, but I was feeling relieved, almost glad, and so was Tom. I could see it in his face. The crime spree was over. He hadn't cracked his knuckles once since his confession.

I wasn't sure about Billy, but I thought he might be looking forward to the new adventure that would come once the police had their hands on us. It was odd, and I didn't understand it, but it was like an unspoken agreement kept us together to face this next challenge: the law.

I'd never been in a police station before, not that I could remember anyway.

I sneaked a look at Billy's calm face and wondered if he knew something about police stations.

There were a bunch of people milling about at a high counter. Staffing the counter were two police officers in blue uniform shirts, no hats. Behind the counter, two more police officers sat at a table, one writing, the other talking on the phone.

We sat on a bench at the back of the room and waited for the hubbub to die down.

After most of the people were gone one of the police officers noticed us. "You waiting to see someone?" He was an older man, with thin gray hair and a ginger, nicotine-stained mustache.

I stepped forward. Billy and Tom followed. The counter came up to my nose. "We've come to confess," I told him.

Billy nodded. "We're turning ourselves in," he said.

Tom cracked his knuckles.

The officer smiled. "Oh, yes? Robbed a bank then, have we?"

"Six," I said.

"Seven," said Billy.

The officer turned to his partner, laughing. "You hear that, Beckett? These kids robbed banks." He pointed. "She robbed six and he robbed seven."

"Thirteen!" his partner cried.

"No," said Tom, "seven in total."

"Oh, well now, seven's not so bad." He laughed.

I held up my bag. "And we're returning the money."

The officer named Beckett took the bag and looked inside. He did a good imitation of fish eyes. "Well, I'll be…!"

The first officer looked in the bag. His grin disappeared. Fish eyes again. "How much money is in here?"

I shrugged. The total wasn't important. Why didn't they arrest us and get it over with?

"Stay right there," Beckett told us. He picked up a phone and spoke into it. Then he hung up and stared at us, shaking his head. "Come with me."

We followed him along a corridor to a door marked *Chief Inspector Teal*. Beckett knocked on the door before pushing it open. Chief Inspector Teal was wearing a dark suit with a green tie. He got up from his desk as we entered. "Sit down," he said. "Could you bring an extra chair, Beckett?"

Officer Beckett put the bag on the Chief Inspector's desk and left. Seconds later, he was back with a chair.

We sat facing the Chief Inspector's desk. Billy was on one side of me, Tom was on the other.

Officer Beckett left again.

"Now what's this all about? You robbed some banks, is that right?" The Chief Inspector used the friendly tone adults often use for children. He smiled at us the way a fond father smiles at clever but naughty kiddies.

I pointed to the bag on the desk. "The money we stole is there, every penny."

The Chief Inspector looked in the bag and then emptied it onto his desk. The bills fell out and formed a paper mountain in the middle of the desk. A few of them fluttered to the floor.

The Chief Inspector's jaw dropped. He stared at us. Then he stared at the money. He stared at us again. He picked up the telephone. "Beckett? Bring in our most recent files on bank robberies, will you!"

$ $ $

Chief Inspector Teal and another plainclothes detective named Sergeant Finch asked a hundred questions, recording our replies on tape.

I thought the questions would never end, but eventually they did. They took us home in a police cruiser. Then they interviewed Joseph and Janice in the living room for almost two hours.

About ten days later, a summons arrived in the mail, ordering us to appear in the juvenile court the following week.

TWENTY-TWO

MAY 22

The judge was a woman with a long narrow nose. She listened to an energetic young man in a gray suit and red tie describe the criminal offences. She watched the shadowy security videos from two of the banks. I could barely make out Billy leaving the bank. It didn't look like him. It could have been anyone wearing glasses and a ballcap.

Then the judge listened to our court-appointed defense counsel, Miss Farthingale, who looked only a few years older than me. She had blond hair to her shoulders and a swishy black suit. She had come to the house a few days ago, asking us more questions.

Miss Farthingale told the judge about the bathroom problem. "The three young defendants, Your Honor, were trying to raise money to have an extra bathroom installed so they would not have to leave their foster home. You see, Your Honor, regulations demand at least two full bathrooms in a house with four children. These children are very close. They did not want to see their family broken up. Staying together was worth any sacrifice to them.

"I would also point out, Your Honor, that the defendants used no weapons of any kind during the robberies. They meant no harm and they deeply regret their actions. The children, the defendants, turned themselves in and returned all the stolen money. Not one penny is missing, Your Honor. One final point, Your Honor: The children saw their cause as a noble one."

"They saw robbing banks as a noble cause?" asked the judge, her eyes widening in disbelief.

"Yes, Your Honor," said Miss Farthingale firmly. "A noble cause indeed. Their intent was to ensure the survival of their family, a family that provides them with love and a sense of belonging, as well as security, all so critically important for young people today. Wouldn't you agree, Your Honor?"

"Hmmph!" said the judge.

Miss Farthingale said, "Your Honor, if the British Columbian Social Services system had been doing its job of looking after the welfare of needy children in this province, there would have been no need for the three defendants to rob banks in the first place."

"They could have been killed or seriously injured," the judge said. "If a security guard or a police officer had started shooting, innocent bystanders might have come to harm as well. Robbing banks is an extremely dangerous game, weapons or not, noble or not." She glared at us from her throne.

I glared back.

Billy looked like he was enjoying himself. His blue eyes sparkled with excitement. Tom was back to cracking his knuckles.

The judge adjourned the case for a week.

$ $ $

A week later, Joseph, Janice and we three delinquents were back in juvenile court. We sat behind a table and waited for the judge to announce her decision.

"First of all," she said, "I want to commend the three of you for your obvious concern for your foster parents, Janice and Joseph Hardy. It reflects well on them as caregivers. Your aim in committing these robberies was to help them. I fully understand that. I also understand that your aim was to help yourselves. You did not want to be taken away from the home and the people you love.

"What I do not understand is why the Hardys' home, which has an excellent history of helping young people, does not receive more support. It is homes like the Hardys' that are so successful in keeping our youth off the streets by providing a safe and nurturing environment.

"I asked my staff to look into the matter, and I can tell you now that emergency funds have been found. The funds to build the extra facility will be provided within the next few months." She paused.

I grinned at her. "Your Honor, does this mean that we won't have to move?"

"Ssshhh," Miss Farthingale whispered. "Her Honor is still speaking."

The judge said, "Yes, young lady. That is precisely what it means."

I turned to my musketeers and we exchanged smiles of relief. I felt like jumping up and yelling, "Three cheers for Her Honor the judge!" right there in the courtroom. I forced myself to be still and quiet.

"Now I will speak of the charges," said the judge, looking at us over her glasses. "Bank robbery is a serious crime. The three of you confessed to the police that you committed seven robberies. You have returned all the money. But you endangered and terrorized the lives of many innocent people. Therefore, you must be punished. You must be made to understand that breaking the law has consequences— *severe* consequences. Nell Ford, Billy Galloway and Tom Okada, please stand."

We stood, shoulder to shoulder, like the Three Musketeers.

I felt as if we were about to be given the death sentence.

The judge took a deep breath. "I have no other choice but to deal with you firmly. I hereby sentence each of you to twenty-eight days in the Vancouver Juvenile Detention Home, starting at the end of the school year, on July third. At the conclusion of your sentence, you will perform three hundred hours of community service. At the rate of ten hours a week, it will take seven months for you to work it off, one month for each bank you terrorized."

$$ \$ \ \$ \ \$ $$

When we got outside in the hallway with Joseph and Janice, I didn't know whether to feel depressed or excited. I said to them, "They'll give you enough money to install the extra bathroom. Now none of us will have to move out, right?"

They smiled happily.

"I can't tell you," Joseph said, "how happy…"

"…it makes us," Janice said.

"Except for—," said Joseph.

"It's great," interrupted Billy, grinning like a maniac.

"Friggin' fantastic," Tom agreed.

Joseph said, "You won't think a month in juvenile detention is so fantastic or..."

"...the three hundred hours of community service," finished Janice. "It's going to be hard work."

"Juvie," I moaned. I knew juvie was not a nice place. "For a whole month!"

Joseph sighed. "It will probably be the hardest month of your life."

"How come?" Tom growled.

"They work you from early morning to night. I've seen it so I know. You'll be mopping floors, cleaning and scrubbing, lifting and carrying— anything and everything. Kitchen work, field work, you name it. You're not going to like it, I promise."

We groaned.

Miss Farthingale joined us. "Don't complain," she said. "It's an extremely light sentence. The judge was easy on you."

"Easy!" said Billy. "What does she do for hard? Send you to Siberia to work on a chain gang?"

"I knew we'd end up in friggin' jail," moaned Tom. He turned to Billy. "I friggin' told you."

But Billy wasn't listening. He seemed stunned. "Plus three hundred hours community work," he groaned.

I said nothing. What could I say? Actually, I was so happy not to be leaving Janice and Joseph that I didn't care about the sentence. I would survive.

TWENTY-THREE

JULY

Before I knew it school was out for the summer and I had to say good-bye to Liesel. I didn't tell her I would be spending most of July in juvie. If I told her she would want to know why, and I had no intention of telling her—or anyone—the long, incredible story. They would think I was making it up.

I told my mom that I was going away on a trip. Some trip.

She probably forgot everything I told her as soon as I was gone. Poor Mom.

On the morning of July 3, Janice and Joseph drove us to what would be our home for the next twenty-eight days: the Juvenile Detention Home. Juvie.

We started saying our good-byes in the lobby.

"A month soon passes, especially if you're busy," said Joseph before they left us. "You're all strong. You'll be fine."

"We'll be back for you on the thirtieth," said Janice, trying to smile. "The house will be so empty without you."

"Think of it as a well-earned holiday for you and Joseph," said Billy.

"You deserve the break from us," agreed Tom.

I was immediately separated from the boys. I felt totally alone. The boys were lucky. At least they had each other.

The less said about juvie the better. I didn't like it, but it could have been worse. Breakfast, as much as you wanted, was at six. If you were late you got nothing. There were eight girls, ranging in age from eleven to sixteen. Joseph was right about the work. It was hard. We started at seven. Everyone was put to work cleaning. The supervisors were strict, but they were fair. I worked mostly in the kitchen and the laundry. Work ended at six. Then it was supper and back to the dormitory, a long room with twenty beds. Lights out was eight o'clock.

For the first week, I ached all over.

Most of the other girls had been there before, some of the hard cases had been there several times. They hassled me because it was my first time. I had a fight after lights out with an older girl. She kept on at me with her foul language. She took a swipe at me, but I ducked. I punched her in the stomach twice and kicked both her shins. The fight was over before it started. The other girls screamed with excitement. They left me alone after that. The night supervisor, a big woman—they were all big women—named Miss Coke, gave us a tongue-lashing. She woke us up at four-thirty the next morning to run around outside in the cold for thirty minutes wearing only our pj's.

Seeing Janice and Joseph when it was all over was like seeing a pair of shining angels. They hugged us. Janice was crying. I was so happy—like Christmas and Easter and my birthday and my mom's birthday all rolled into one.

Tom had a black eye and a band-aid on his forehead but he was grinning like he'd just won the lightweight boxing championship of the world.

It looked to me like Billy had enjoyed being in jail. He was an inch taller and looked like he'd completed a triumphant exploration in the jungles of darkest Africa.

TWENTY-FOUR

Saturday night, a week later, I was sitting on my bed trying to brush the juvie out of my hair and mind.

"Will you brush my hair when you're finished?" Lisa asked. Janice would be taking her to the hospital on Monday for her operation.

Right now, she was sitting on her bed, Pumpkin in her lap.

"Of course. I'd love to brush your hair. Want me to braid it? It would look so cool with lots of little braids."

"Sure," she said, absentmindedly patting Pumpkin's back. "Do you think getting my tonsils out will hurt? I'm really scared."

"Don't be scared, Lisa. Once your tonsils are out, no more sore throats. And you get as much Jell-O and ice cream as you want."

"Just thinking about the operation scares me. But the worst part is I'll have to stay overnight at the hospital. All alone." Her eyes filled with tears.

I held her and she buried her face in my shoulder.

"I sure missed you when you were away," she murmured. "And the boys. I missed them too. But I missed you the most."

She felt small and thin, like her bones were twigs. "And I missed you," I told her, patting her back. "You shouldn't worry. I'm sure the operation will be quick. They'll put you to sleep so you won't feel a thing."

"Are you sure?"

"I'm positive. And when you wake up, we'll all be there. Janice and Joseph and the boys and me. Our whole family."

"Promise?" she said, rubbing her nose on her pajama sleeve and sniffing.

"Everything is going to be all right, Kiddo. I promise."

$ $ $

Showering and scrubbing took me longer now that I was coming home smelling of horses. I tried to get home for a shower before the others so I wouldn't have to put up with rude comments like, "Phew! Did someone sit on a skunk or something?" from Tom.

It was great having that extra bathroom. Janice and Joseph had surprised us with the new bathroom when we got home from juvie.

My job was cleaning out the stalls and brushing the police horses. I actually didn't mind it. I loved the horses and loved learning about them. They were starting to recognize me, especially when I brought carrots or apples for treats. I got to work with a nice First Nations woman named Denise. I was lucky. I had the best job out of the three of us.

Billy worked at the recycling depot, sorting glass, plastic, newspapers and cardboard. He came home filthy too, though he didn't smell as bad as I did.

Tom's job was the worst. He had to scrub pots and pans in the kitchen at Burnaby General Hospital.

"Filthy smelly pots," he complained when we were hanging out in the boys' room one night. "Downright disgusting."

"Hey, Tom, my man," Billy said. "You want to trade jobs halfway through? I'll do your job at the hospital. And you do mine at the recycling depot. All that fresh air and sunshine, you'd love it."

"You'd do that? You'd trade with me?"

"Sure thing. What are friends for?" Billy leaned over and gave him the two-fisted Musketeers salute. He turned to me. "What's family for? Right, Nails?"

"Right on. All for one and one for all," I said, grinning at him. "By the way, I've gone back to my real name. No more Nails, okay?"

Tom's eyebrows disappeared under his spiky hair. "No more Nails?"

"I like Nell," Billy said and gave me one of his sweet smiles.

If I hadn't been lounging on the orange beanbag, I probably would have melted right there.

"Nell is a good name," said Tom, nodding thoughtfully, as if there had been some doubt. "My father used to say, 'We learn little from victory, much from defeat.'"

I looked at Billy. Billy looked at me. "What's victory and defeat got to do with me changing my name back to Nell?"

Tom shrugged. "I'm not sure."

Billy laughed. Then I laughed, and Tom joined in.

After everything that had happened, I was ready for my real name. I'd worn Nails long enough. It was time to be me again.

Acknowledgments

Grateful thanks to our editor, Melanie Jeffs, for her patience and hard work.

JAMES HENEGHAN is the best-selling author of dozens of books for kids and young adults, including *Safe House* and *Waiting for Sarah*.

NORMA CHARLES has written many books for kids, including *The Accomplice*, shortlisted for the Sheila A. Egoff Children's Literature Prize.

Norma and James both live in Vancouver, British Columbia. *Bank Job* was inspired by a newspaper account of three teens who robbed seven banks in the Vancouver area.